THE FOREST CITY

Trevor Holliday

Barnstork Press

ISBN-13: 9798371773081
ISBN-10: 1477123456

Cover design by: John M. Holliday
Library of Congress Control Number: 2018675309
Printed in the United States of America

This book is dedicated to the late Richard D. Peters
Great American
My teacher and mentor

CONTENTS

A GROOVY KIND OF LOVE

Hal Bailey loved early winter. Hal didn't care if his love for the shoulder season was cliché. He liked the colors and smells of late fall. Football games. Leaves changing colors.

But winter? Winter was different. Hal loved the anticipation of the Christmas season. The lights, the store windows, the songs. All contributed to Hal's feeling of bonhomie.

"You're sentimental, Hal," Gerry Joyce, said. "You're a sentimental man."

Hal looked at Gerry. As if Gerry himself wasn't sentimental.

Gerry Joyce stood behind the counter in his shop on Prospect Avenue wearing a gray *GARDA* sweatshirt. Cigars and Zippo lighters lined up under the glass counter. Guns, ammunition, mace, brass knuckles, knife combs. All those were also available, but locked in the back room.

Gerry could weep over a picture of a kitten playing with a ball of yarn, and sometimes he did.

"Maybe I am sentimental," Hal said, "you think

this is a problem?"

"I think it's refreshing, lad," Gerry said. "I think you should go and make a night of it. You're only young for so long."

Hal loved the fall months, but September, October, and November were finished. Autumn was kaput. Fall was for football games, leaves falling, festive food. But fall was over.

Outside Gerry's shop, near the corner of East 4th Street and Prospect Avenue, scraps of paper blew east then west as though trying to decide upon their direction. Pigeons worked against the wind. The temperature in Cleveland had dropped and was going to drop more. Action 5 news predicted snow.

Winter was as good as here. If Hal hadn't been in such a good mood he would have seen the first signs of snow and remembered how the festive season was inevitably followed by unending gray months.

Hal's mind wasn't only on the changing season, though.

Hal was taking out Angie Mandarich tonight.

* * *

The date with Angie was a long time coming. Hal was going to pick Angie up at the Tender Trap Men's Salon where she worked, then drive downtown to Eddie Swanson's Forest City for dinner before the movie.

North by Northwest was showing at the Heights Art Theater.

Angie had never seen the movie. Hal mentioned it to Angie when she was styling his hair a few weeks ago. She had Sonny and Cher on the stereo at the Tender Trap singing *A Groovy Kind of Love*. Hal liked it as much as The Mindbender's version.

"It's Alfred Hitchcock, right?" Angie said.

"It's the one where Cary Grant gets chased by a crop-duster," Hal said. "He's running down a road in South Dakota or somewhere. I'm pretty sure it's South Dakota, because Mount Rushmore is in there somewhere. Anyway, it's Cary Grant, so naturally, he's wearing a gray flannel suit, but the thing barely gets smudged even though he's out in the middle of nowhere surrounded by corn fields. You've never seen it? You'll like it."

"They used to show some wild movies at that place," she said. "You're sure you're not taking me to something dirty? Like Cybill Shepherd in *Taxi Driver*?"

"Uhn-uh," Hal said. "You talking to me?"

"Nobody else here," Angie said.

"It's a little sexy maybe," Hal said. "The movie is. Especially at the end. I'd rate it M."

"They say PG now, Hal," Angie said. "They don't use M anymore. They haven't for years and years. Where have you been?"

"Sure, I know, but I like M better," Hal said. "It's a lot more descriptive. I mean, what does parental guidance even mean? Depends on the parents.

Plus, who needs a bunch of kids sitting in the movie theater with you?"

"You sure you don't want more off the back?" she said. Angie was a good stylist. She didn't push. She knew Hal liked the modified Prince Valiant razor-cut style he'd adopted. His hair was mostly grown back since his Arizona trip, but there were still patches of skin on the back of his neck lacking pigmentation from the sun exposure.

Angie was making the best of it.

"Do it the way you think," he said. "You know best. You're the pro."

"That's a funny answer coming from you," Angie said. "You usually are so specific."

"Maybe I'm turning over a new leaf," Hal said. "Starting early for the new year."

Hal wondered if she was going to offer him one of the whiskey sours. He liked them. It was one of the first things he liked about the Tender Trap besides, obviously, Angie. It wasn't just the whiskey sour. It was the way she made them. The whole thing was very sexy in a classy way Hal liked.

"I was thinking maybe you could put in a perm," Angie said. "Lotta guys are doing that, and it looks pretty good on some of them. It's low-care. No fuss, no muss."

Angie ran her fingers through Hal's hair. He was thinking he should just ask her about the whiskey sour since he was under the impression the drink was part of the deal. On the other hand, he didn't want to push things. Mitch Walczak had come in here and gotten his hair cut by Angie. Hal wouldn't even call what Mitch got a hairstyle on account of Mitch only had the fringe around his big bald dome.

Mitch hadn't been offered a whiskey sour by Angie and he let Hal know about that.

"Jeez, Hal," Mitch said. "Your girlfriend treated me like hired help. I'm not kidding."

Angie was taking her time with Hal.

"You got good strong hair," she said. "Very healthy in the roots department."

"How long's it take to do?" Hal said. "I gotta think about it."

"Depends," she said. "Anyway, what time are you picking me up?"

 Six o'clock?"

"Five if you're picking me up here," she said.

Hal wasn't nervous until this morning. He planned for months to ask her out. Ever since she'd started cutting his hair. *Styling* his hair.

But then he had gone on the business trip out of town which lasted longer and had been more complicated than Hal expected. After the trip, even when he was in the Tender Trap getting his hair styled, the time never seemed right. But when the conversation about the movie arose, it just seemed natural for Hal to ask her.

Angie, sounding like she wondered why he waited so long, said sure.

* * *

He told Gerry Joyce the story. Gerry, lighting a cigar, nodded his head.

"She's the one looks like the daughter on that show?" he said. "Adrienne Whatever-her-name-is?"

"Barbeau," Hal said. "Adrienne Barbeau. Yeah, Angie gets that a lot."

"So you've said, lad," Gerry said. "Beautiful. Go and have a grand time."

* * *

After their dinner and movie last night, the next morning Hal lay in bed. He was in no hurry to get up.

He hadn't picked up Angie Mandarich at the Tender Trap. Instead, she called him last minute, asking Hal to pick her up at her home. She told Hal that as of a couple of days ago, she was living with her mother, and her two older brothers, Stan and Ted, back in the house where she'd grown up.

"I mean, Merry Christmas, right?" she said.

Hal said he thought Angie lived in an apartment with a couple of roommates. Something like *Apartment 3G*.

It *had* been kinda like that, Angie said.

"This is just temporary until I get another place,"

she said. "Turns out one of them, Karen? The one we gave rent money to? Turns out she has a little problem with cocaine. Can you believe it? We had no idea."

"Sometimes with cocaine, it's hard to tell," Hal said.

"We had no idea until we were locked out of our place. I mean it's embarrassing, and inconvenient, and all. I can't even imagine what was going through her mind."

"Sounds like she had more than a little problem. Did you get your things out of the place?"

"Oh, the guy had everything in U-Haul boxes," Angie said. "We just had to go through it all, me and Donna. The part that's kind of icky is thinking about the landlord packing it up. I mean he's just a little creepy."

"You need my help, just let me know," Hal said. "That's kinda my bread and butter."

"You're sweet," Angie said. "I'll see you at the house at six."

❀ ❀ ❀

Angie's mother came out of the kitchen to get a look at Hal.

"Mom, this is Hal. I've told you about him."

"The one with the hair," her mother said. "Just get home early, Angie. We got stuff to do tomorrow."

Stan Mandarich came in from the back room. He

held a copy of *Death of a Salesman* in his left hand. He looked like he could fill-in as a lineman for the Browns. Maybe two linemen. Stan Mandarich gave Hal a firm handshake after looking him over.

"How's the part look, Stan?" Angie said.

"Pretty good," Stan said, "But I gotta say I might be a little old for Biff."

Hal was six foot four. Stan towered over Hal, and was built like the side of beef Rocky Balboa took jabs at in Burt Young's meat locker.

"Stan's auditioning," Angie said. "He's an actor."

"You played for Heights, didn't you," Stan said.

"Couple years," Hal said.

"Good times back then," Stan said. "We should talk sometime."

Angie gave Hal a quick kiss in the car.

"That's my family," she said. "One big happy family. Except you haven't met Ted yet. Ted's the oldest. He's probably at church. He's kinda religious."

Hal turned the key in the ignition.

"Ted's bigger than Stan," Angie said. "Just so you know."

Hal nodded. Stan and Ted.

"They wrestle," she said. "Well, they used to wrestle. You wouldn't recognize them anyway, though. They always used to wear these masks. Mom wouldn't let them wrestle without the masks. She said she would be mortified. They were going to be called the Masked Magicians."

"Maybe I used to see them," Hal said. "You know

Mitch Walczak, right? He used to get tickets from work for down at the Arena. Barons, Cavaliers, all that, before they built the Coliseum out there in Richfield. Plus he always had it on Channel 43 Saturday morning if I went over there."

Angie shook her head.

"Their career didn't really go anywhere," she said. "They're just big pussycats most of the time. Plus, a lot of that stuff is kinda choreographed, you know?"

Hal nodded. Lions were big pussycats too.

"They couldn't get their parts right," Angie said. "The promoter is a nice guy, he really is, even though on television he's always screaming into the microphone. He's the one wears the fez? Did you ever see him?"

"Oh yeah," Hal said. "You're talking about the Mysterious Pharaoh, right? He's supposed to be Egyptian."

Angie nodded.

"His real name was Mike Koory. Anyway, he was apologetic as hell. He kept telling Stan he thought he and Ted had some ring potential."

"They did wrestle a couple times, didn't they? Couple matches? I'm thinking I mighta seen them once or twice. I kinda remember the Masked Magician thing. Maybe they were up against The Love Brothers or somebody. Pampero Firpo? Somebody like that. The Big Cat, Ernie Ladd? I don't know."

"Funny you should mention Pampero Firpo,"

9

Angie said. "I actually met him. Very nice guy. You'd never recognize him. I saw him at Higbees, and I only would have known it was him because Mike was there. Mike Koory, like I said. I was with Ted down there doing Christmas shopping. I was pretty little, I guess. Anyway, Ted sees Mike and Mike introduces us and Pampero Firpo leans over and he starts talking to me. Asking me what I wanted for Christmas. I mean, I don't even know what I told him. Probably a Barbie or something. Later on Ted told me who the guy was and then he showed me a picture of this crazy looking guy. *The Wild Bull of the Pampas*. You wouldn't have guessed any of that if you saw him talking to me that day at Higbees."

"So what happened to your brothers and their wrestling?"

"They had a few matches," Angie said. "Still, it's kinda crazy. Maybe ironic is a better word. I was pretty little back then, so I didn't know exactly what was going on, but my mother explained it to me later. I mean, Mike basically fired them because they don't know their moves and he's afraid somebody might get hurt, but still, they're *supposed* to act like they're killing each other out there."

"Yeah, sure," Hal said, "but like you said, it's all choreographed. Nobody's getting creamed out there."

"Like a ballet," she said.

"Yeah," Hal said, "but more entertaining, you ask

me."

"Now, Stan's been getting parts in plays. Turns out he's really good, except with his size he always gets certain parts. But you should have seen him in *You Can't Take it With You*. He played Boris Kolenkhov. He's the Russian dancing instructor. I mean, here's Stan, all six foot eight of him. And he has a great Russian accent. He's really good. Everybody says he should get in movies."

"Your family isn't Russian, though, is it?" Hal said.

Angie looked at him.

"No way," she said. "Polish all the way. Mom's got a picture of Bobby Vinton in the kitchen.

"*The Polish Prince*," Hal said. "*Moja droga, ja cię kocham*, right?"

"That's sweet," Angie said. "You said it just right, I think. Mom's gonna love you."

They didn't talk for a minute. They were still sitting in the front seat of Hal's car. Hal was letting Angie's family situation sink in.

She socked him on his arm, but friendly.

"Hey," she said, "are we going out on a date, or what?"

Hal looked over at her. He made a show of rubbing his arm. She was smiling.

"You like something really nice?" he said.

"Of course I do," Angie said. "Why wouldn't I like something really nice?"

❊ ❊ ❊

11

Hal got out of bed. He was still thinking about the evening. Things had gone well. He had taken Angie to Eddie Swanson's Forest City. That set him back a couple of bucks, but it was worth it. The dinner was good. Angie ordered a chef salad and Hal had the prime rib medium rare.

He introduced Angie to Vic Collister, the piano player.

Vic was a good guy. He played the Mannix theme when Hal came in.

"Wow, Hal," Vic said. "You're dating this beautiful lady?"

"I didn't know you were taking me to the Forest City, Hal," Angie said. "This place is really uptown. I gotta say I'm impressed."

Hal nodded. Gratified. He had considered the Swabian Club, but figured German would be too heavy.

And for Angie? Hal wanted to go all out.

So Eddie Swanson's Forest City got the nod. White tablecloths and all.

They split a slice of New York cheesecake for dessert. Two forks. How about that?

Angie liked *North by Northwest*. Who doesn't?

"Cary Grant is so cool," Angie said. "He's flat on his face in the cornfield but he barely gets flustered."

Hal got Angie home early.

Even while he walked her up the steps to her house, Hal couldn't help thinking about Stan and Ted Mandarich.

Ted was home when Hal brought Angie home. The one Angie said was religious.

Ted was sitting in the living room drinking a cup of tea. Hal didn't know what he had been expecting, the guy was going to be sitting there on the couch wearing a monk's robe? Ted looked like a regular guy. Just big.

Ted and Stan would be protective of their sister, though. Even if they had been a big flop in professional wrestling, they could still flatten Hal like a potato latke.

Stan and Ted together probably outweighed Hal by a couple hundred pounds.

Hal was quick, but quick wouldn't be nearly enough against the Mandarich behemoths.

Still, it had been a great evening.

Angie gave Hal a kiss in the hall when he left.

"I forgot to put up the mistletoe," she said.

"Too bad," Hal said. He kissed her and that made about four times he had kissed her, counting the ones in the car. This one lasted for a while.

"Call me again," she said.

There was no reason to worry about Angie's brothers.

EARLY CHRISTMAS TINSEL

Eddie Swanson's Forest City was swinging.

Jimmy Frank Waters was filling in behind the bar.

Piano music came in from the dining room where Vic Collister played the hits. Here in the bar the tips were good. After all, it *was* the holiday season.

Hank Standish who was standing on the rail down the bar reminded Jimmy Frank of Clark Clifford and that made him think about the Johnson brothers.

Hank Standish looked like Clark Clifford.

Truth was, Jimmy Frank didn't give a damn about either Hank Standish or Clark Clifford.

But Jimmy Frank *definitely* had a grudge against the Johnson brothers.

And Jimmy Frank was going to do something about them.

Marvel and Arthur Johnson were identical twins.

They ran poker games around the city and fenced stolen property out of a combined insurance office and funeral supply store near 105th Street.

Thinking about the Johnson brothers bothered the hell out of Jimmy Frank.

This was what had happened:

Jimmy Frank wasn't in love with collections, but like bartending, he could do the job if he had to.

The Johnson brothers had given Jimmy Frank a job a week and a half ago.

Clark Clifford, a white Brecksville insurance man and a racetrack regular, had gotten roped into a card game run by the Johnson brothers.

That was Clifford's first mistake. There's a world of difference between making two dollar bets at Thistledown and dropping money at an inner city card game run by the Johnson brothers. Clark Clifford had gotten in way over his head.

Clifford's second mistake occurred when he couldn't cover his bets immediately.

Clifford accepted a short-term loan from the Johnson brothers.

The Johnson brothers loved making loans.

His third mistake was letting several days pass without coming up from his home in Brecksville to pay off the debt.

Everybody knew the Johnson brothers.

Unfortunately for Clifford, he was too naive to understand what he'd gotten himself into.

Marvel Johnson's instructions to Jimmy Frank were clear:

"You wanna give this dude something to remember," Marvel said. "I know you know how to do this. Don't leave too many marks, but let him know he don't mess with me and my brother."

Jimmy Frank nodded.

The next day, Jimmy Frank called upon Clark Gifford in his Brecksville office.

Right across from the gazebo in the town square.

Downtown Brecksville looked like one of the Andy Hardy movies Jimmy Frank used to watch when he was a kid. It looked like the kind of place with a malt shop across from the town library.

Clifford's receptionist looked up from a novel. Saw Jimmy Frank.

Jimmy Frank smiled at her. He didn't give her a chance to ask him if she could be of assistance or whatever the hell else she was supposed to say.

He went straight back to Clifford's office before she could tell the man he was coming.

Pictures of Clifford's family and Rotary awards were hung on the wall along with early Christmas tinsel. There was a cute girl wearing braces on top of a horse and a boy in a coonskin cap.

Jimmy Frank looked at the pictures and then looked at Clark Gifford.

"How are you doing, Clark?" he said. "I'm here on behalf of the Johnson brothers."

Jimmy Frank smiled. Amiably.

You could do this a few ways. Jimmy Frank figured he'd try the easy way first.

Clifford reached for the telephone on his desk.

Jimmy Frank took the receiver away from him. Told him exactly why he had come to see him.

"You work for them?" Clifford said. The man looked surprisingly calm.

"Long drive down here, Mr. Clifford," Jimmy Frank said. He looked at the family pictures again. Clifford's wife looked a lot like Donna Reed. "I hate to have to come down here more than once."

Clifford was cooperative.

"Just a second," Clifford said. He looked around on his desk like he had misplaced something. "I meant to call them. I really did. It was on my to-do list. I don't want any trouble. I have the money right here."

Jimmy Frank got a little nervous for a moment when Clifford reached into his desk.

Like this was gonna be the part where Clifford brought out a cannon and pointed it at Jimmy Frank's chest.

Jimmy Frank could have done something right then, but he didn't.

Clifford didn't give him a chance. When his hand came back out of the desk he was holding a bank envelope decorated with red poinsettias. The envelope was fat with bills like he was being generous with the United Way.

Fifteen crisp one hundred dollar bills, fresh from the bank. They were so fresh, Jimmy Frank had a problem counting them first time around. But they were all there. Jimmy Frank kept ten bills in the envelope for the brothers.

He kept five for himself. The agreed upon terms.

Jimmy Frank didn't have to lay a hand on Clifford. He was feeling good when he took the money to the Johnson brothers that evening. No sense in breaking a man's arm when he's giving you the money as nice as Clifford did.

Arthur Johnson looked stern when Jimmy Frank arrived with the cash

"You need to show me *all* the money," Arthur said.

Jimmy Frank shook his head. There was no need to show Arthur Johnson the other five hundred.

That money was his.

"Bring out the rest. There should be an extra five in there."

From behind his back, Jimmy Frank heard Marvel's voice.

There was something about the way Marvel said the words.

Jimmy Frank turned around.

Marvel Johnson was pointing a nickel-plated automatic at Jimmy Frank.

"We didn't send you down to Mayberry to pick up the mail, Jimmy Frank. You were *sent* to give the man a lesson," Marvel said. "Clark Clifford give me a call two hours ago. Tells me how he sent you off with the money. Man sounded just as fresh as can be. He wanted to make sure me and my brother had no hard *feelings*."

"You got your money," Jimmy Frank said. "What do you care about how I got it?"

Marvel pushed the gun into Jimmy Frank's neck.

"Gimme the rest," he said. "Your job was to give Howdy Doody a message. What kinda message you give him? Me and my brother don't run some kinda savings and loan. When a man thinks he can pick and choose when to pay his debt? Word like that gets around."

"People begin to say we soft," Arthur said.

Jimmy Frank handed Arthur the rest of the money.

"My brother's right. We are anything but soft," Marvel said. "Next time, we'll send somebody to bomb the place."

He lowered the gun.

Arthur Johnson peeled two twenty dollar bills from his money clip.

"There you go, Jimmy Frank," Arthur said. "Take this for your gas and time."

Jimmy Frank stood in front of the brothers. Looked at the bills.

Forty dollars.

Arthur and Marvel stood in front of him. The twins wore matching fur-trimmed plaid overcoats. Marvel's green, Arthur's lavender.

Four hundred and sixty dollars short of the five hundred they agreed to pay Jimmy Frank.

"You can let yourself out, Jimmy Frank," Marvel said.

Jimmy Frank dropped the bills on the floor. He left.

The Johnson brothers were laughing. Jimmy

Frank heard them all the way out the door.

Days later, Jimmy Frank was still angry.

Jimmy Frank looked at Hank Standish standing at the bar. This man knew how to talk. Talking and talking. Looking more and more like Clark Clifford.

Jimmy Frank shook his head. He was going to have to *do* something about Marvel and Arthur Johnson.

Tomorrow he would get in touch with Herman Taylor. Herm knew the Johnson brothers better than Jimmy Frank. Maybe Herm would have an idea what to do about Jimmy Frank's problem.

THE EXPANDING MAN

Vic Collister, lounge pianist at Eddie Swanson's Forest City, knew all about Eggy.

Vic had heard the Eggy Eglington story several times from Eggy himself.

He had heard enough to know Williston "Eggy" Eglington III had it made.

Eggy had all the money a person could ever ask for.

Not that there weren't reasonable checks to Eggy's wealth.

Eggy's uncle knew his nephew's habits well, and the terms of Eggy's trust were unbreakable. He might not not have access to all of his money, but Eggy would never go completely broke.

Still, Eggy blew more money in an average month than most people see in a year.

But then on the first business day of the next month? Presto.

Eggy was back in business.

With no credit cards, no debts, no alimony payments, Eggy's life was simple.

The uncle also made sure Eggy's rent at the Alhambra Hotel was paid *in perpetuum.*

Eggy would never find himself out on the street, no matter what he did.

Eggy had nothing to worry about, although things often got thin for Eggy at the end of the month.

At the end of each month, Eggy sometimes would find himself cash poor. Then, out came the Dinty Moore stew and cranberry juice he kept in the cupboards of his apartment. Eggy would have to wait until the start of the new month to enjoy porterhouse steaks and Old Fashioneds again.

So, there really was no need to feel sorry for Eggy Eglington.

Eggy had it made.

Still, Vic felt sorry for Eggy.

Eddie Swanson's Forest City was Eggy's favorite joint.

The bar and grill were located around the corner from where the Roxy Theater used to stand on Short Vincent.

❊ ❊ ❊

Eggy liked chatting with Vic. Eggy thought Vic knew everything.

Somewhere, Eggy got the idea Vic knew about all the underworld characters who had come in and out of this place and others during Short Vincent's heyday.

"You know where the skeletons are hidden, don't you Vic?" Eggy said. "You know all about these *bombings*."

Vic quickly put a finger to his lips before returning it to the piano.

No reason to talk about *bombings*. There had been enough of those. No good could come from their discussion.

Eggy liked sitting near the piano. He liked enjoying his strip steak, grilled rare, and his baked potato while listening to Vic play.

Right now, Vic was playing Steely Dan.

Deacon Blues

The song was a little departure for Vic. Maybe just a little edgy, but it was early in the evening.

What the heck?

This is the day of the expanding man

Everyone knew Eddie Swanson's would not survive much longer. Progress had changed everything and Eddie Swanson's was a stubborn holdout.

Tonight, Eggy wore a red plaid jacket, light green pleated shirt, and a tie dotted with poinsettias.

Eggy had never gotten over the Roxy being razed, even though the landmark's destruction had occurred a few years before.

"What a show they use to put on," Eggy said. "Boy, were those girls talented?"

Vic nodded.

"I don't care what anyone says," Eggy said. "It took a pile of talent to put on a burlesque show like they put on. Plus, they had live comics and musicians. Am I right Vic?"

Vic nodded.

"You ever play burlesque, Vic?" Eggy said. "I mean, that was live music, wasn't it? You play in a house band? Bada bing, bada boom."

Eggy pantomimed a drummer's rim shot.

Vic shook his head.

"That was before my time, Eggy," Vic said. "You might as well be asking me if I played in Vaudeville."

"Aw, c'mon," Eggy said, "What are you saying? You're not that much younger than me, are you?"

"No, you're right," Vic said. "You're right."

It wasn't the first time Eggy had asked him the same question about burlesque.

Vic liked Eggy. Eggy was a trip.

"It was a shame the place went downhill," Eggy said. "They shouldn't have taken it down though."

"You're right," Vic said.

"The Roxy was history."

Eggy was a walking target for con men. It worried Vic, but only a little.

Eggy was a big boy, wasn't he?

He could take care of himself.

NOBODY DOES IT BETTER

Jackie Dunne, twenty-seven years old, thought about Phil Fontana's offer.

Jackie liked his job parking cars at Easy Al's Five Dollar Parking.

Conn Rutherford was Jackie's boss at the parking lot. Conn and Jackie had a deal.

Conn told Jackie that Easy Al, who owned the place, didn't know how many cars were parked in the lot on any given day.

The more cars Jackie moved in, the more money he made.

Conn was a funny guy. Kept a photo of Shelly Fabares on the wall from the sixties. Drank Strohs from the can in the shack. Conn was a real beer lover. He looked older than the sixty-four years old his license said. Just for the hell of it, Jackie had looked at Conn's license once when Conn was out.

Sixty-four years old.

Jackie didn't want to be sitting in a parking lot shack when *he* was sixty-four.

But the job Phil Fontana was talking about was

different.

Phil Fontana.

Fontana had dropped his card and a ten dollar bill into Jackie Dunne's hand the first time he saw him. *Before* Jackie had parked his car.

They had only talked for a couple minutes, but a couple minutes was all Fontana needed, as fast as he talked.

"This is just a sweet side-hustle I'm offering you," Fontana said.

Jackie had parked Fontana's brown Dodge Challenger. Worked the car out of the back of the lot. Shifting the Challenger into reverse, gunning the accelerator, slamming the brakes. Leaving inches to spare in front of the next car. Nice car with the Hurst shifter and the big 426 hemi under the hood. Jackie liked the car even more than the similar Barracuda.

Phil Fontana was perched next to the shack, slapping his pigskin gloves together.

Fontana puffed on his briar pipe, waiting for Jackie to get back to the shack.

Conn wasn't there. He was on his mid-morning break at the High-Lite Bar. He wouldn't be back soon.

Before leaving, Conn always turned the space heater down to the lowest setting.

The shack was icy.

Entering the shack with Fontana, Jackie Dunne pushed the heater's dial to high. A whine came from the green appliance. The coils turned white-orange.

Phil Fontana looked at the heater.

"You don't know physics, do you?" Fontana said.

Jackie shook his head.

"Simple thermodynamics," Fontana said. "It's gonna cost a helluva lot more to start your heater than if you just leave it run."

Jackie shrugged. He didn't give a shit about the electric bill or about thermodynamics. He was cold.

Eventually, the shack would warm up.

"Phil Fontana," Fontana said.

Jackie shook his hand.

"You're gonna wanna turn it down," Fontana said, pointing at the heater. "Down, but not all the way off. Somewhere in the middle. It's what you call the sweet spot."

The shack was starting to heat.

Fontana knocked his pipe against the heater.

"I can't help but noticing this heater. It's an unusual model," he said. "Montgomery Ward, I wanna say just postwar. They sold everything at one time. Still, at the end of the day, they were never more than a low-grade Sears Roebuck."

❋ ❋ ❋

Phil Fontana said he liked the way Jackie backed the Challenger into the narrow spot.

Jackie performed the stunt at high speed, practically without looking.

"No kidding," Fontana said. "I've seen a lot of drivers. Nobody backs a car into a spot the way you just did. Like Debby Boone says, kid, *Nobody Does it Better*. Plus, you're working at high speed. You sure your name ain't Jackie *Stewart*?"

Fontana, schmoozing. Pipe clenched between his teeth.

Jackie was pretty sure Debby Boone didn't sing *Nobody Does it Better*.

Maybe Carly Simon. It wasn't Jackie's kind of music, but the radio in the shack belonged to Conn, and so Conn controlled the dial.

Either way, this Phil Fontana wasn't a guy you could easily interrupt.

"You can't teach that kinda driving confidence," Fontana said. "You can't even begin to teach it. I watched you hard. I was saying to myself it's just like Wolfgang Amadeus Mozart himself is parking these cars."

Jackie looked at Fontana.

Fontana wasn't finished.

"You telling me nobody taught you how to park cars like that?"

"Uhn-uh," Jackie said. "Nobody showed me how to do anything. I just always been able to do it."

"You any good behind the wheel outside the lot? Once you get on the open road?"

Jackie nodded his head. Jackie knew how to drive better than anyone he knew.

"I never heard any complaints," Jackie said.

Wondering what Fontana was leading up to.

"I just got the knack, I guess," Jackie said.

Fontana was looking at Jackie. Assessing him.

"I got some jobs I need a driver for," Fontana said. "I'd try you out on one or two jobs, they could lead to more if you play your cards right."

Play your cards right.

One or two jobs. Maybe more later depending on how things worked out.

"I need a guy who can drive and not ask questions," Fontana said. "Is that something you can handle?"

Jackie was interested.

Most days at Easy Al's were the same-old same-old.

Parking cars was easy for Jackie. Just like a high-speed jigsaw puzzle. He didn't even have to think about it. Just a quick glance over his shoulder.

The clientele was something else. Businessmen coming in, throwing their keys at Jackie. Acting like they were Prince Ranier of Monaco. Guys like that, they didn't tip. Truth was, hardly anybody tipped at Easy Al's.

You gotta make your money in volume, Conn said.

Fontana said he needed a driver. Hinted about money. Said he didn't like paying people below a couple hundred a job.

"Meet me tomorrow afternoon," Fontana said. "You off at four?

"Three," Jackie said.

Conn didn't care if Jackie took off early. The

afternoon would be slow.

"Fine," Fontana said. "Dandy. Drive me around the town. Like an audition."

Fontana looked at Jackie again. Scrutinizing him.

"Nice if you cut the hair, but at least you gotta lose the beads," Fontana said. "Steinbrenner don't let the Yanks go hippie and neither do I."

"This isn't a chauffeur gig, is it?" Jackie said. "What difference do the beads make?"

Jackie wasn't going to wear a monkey suit. No plain black suit like an undertaker for Jackie.

Fontana shook his head.

"Uhn-uh," he said. "I don't need a chauffeur. Listen, do I gotta remind you about the part where you don't ask too many questions?"

Jackie shook his head. He held his palms up toward Fontana.

Fontana looked at him. Handed Jackie another twenty.

"Where am I supposed to meet you?" Jackie said.

Fontana told Jackie to meet him outside Municipal Stadium. Under the big Chief Wahoo sign.

"You're gonna give me a ride around," Fontana said, "I wanna see what you can do. But one thing I *don't* want you to do is to get pulled over."

Fontana was serious.

"I don't like getting pulled over, Jackie," he said. "That's where the haircut comes in. Fuzz don't dig longhairs. Getting pulled over is something I really don't like."

WOMEN'S DEPARTMENT AT THE THOM MCAN SHOE STORE

Jimmy Frank went to Herman Taylor's place of employment the next morning.

Herm "the Germ" Taylor.

Herm and Jimmy Frank went way back. They used to sneak into Kung Fu movies at the Scrumpy Dump Theater on Euclid Avenue when they were both coming up. Herm knew the streets like no other.

If Herm couldn't offer Jimmy Frank a solution, there was no solution to be found.

Currently, Herm worked in the women's department at the Thom McAn on St. Clair. It seemed funny to Jimmy Frank how Herm showed up day-in-day-out at Thom McAn, but he didn't think anything of calling Jimmy Frank to ask for him to fill in for him at Eddie Swanson's.

The shoe store was busy on account of Christmas being around the corner.

Jimmy Frank watched Herm struggling under a stack of at least six shoe boxes, trying to keep them from toppling on a lady customer.

Jimmy Frank picked up a shoe from a display table. Flipped it over to look at the tag.

Herm made a couple quick downward signals with his free hand when he went by.

Motioning Jimmy Frank to wait.

"I gotta customer, brother," Herm said. "Why you coming down here? You gonna have to wait until my smoke break. Go ahead and look round the store. Just don't make no trouble for me."

Jimmy Frank nodded. He was here to ask Herman some advice, he could play by the man's rules.

He put the first shoe down and moved a few steps away.

Close enough to hear Herm, far enough to maintain discretion.

Herm's lady customer was struggling with an instep problem. Fitting her with fashionable pumps would be tricky.

"It started with a bunion," the woman said. "I been to I don't know how many podiatrists. None of them do nothing for me. Plus, the bunions ain't even on the same side of my feet. Then, top things off, I get this hammertoe. Prolly the fault of the podiatrist, but I'm gonna let that go. I'm just letting that one go completely. Thing is, I *gotta* wear pretty shoes when I go out at night or I might as well die."

Jimmy Frank watched Herm shake his head. Listening to the lady.

Normally, Herm Taylor was a smooth operator. This time, though, he brought brown shoes with wooden heels out of the back room. Offering them to the woman.

What the hell was Herm thinking?

Jimmy Frank wasn't a shoe pro, but even he knew this was going to be a problem.

This woman was gonna want *pretty* shoes. She didn't want wooden heels.

"These will solve your problem," Herm said. "Designed with a situation like you got without losing style sense."

Jimmy Frank shook his head.

Herm, acting like he was holding Cinderella's glass slipper.

The woman gave a why-are-you-messing-with-me laugh.

"You *trying* to be funny, Herman Taylor? I don't want *clogs*," she said. "You bring me out something *pretty* and I'll try them on. I don't want nothing to do with these wooden boats."

The lady had a point as far as Jimmy Frank was concerned.

This was a decent looking woman, but wearing plain orthopedic shoes, especially brown shoes with wooden heels was going to put her at a social disadvantage. Herm should have known better.

While Herm Taylor brought more shoes to the woman, Jimmy Frank looked at a pair of alligators.

Jimmy Frank was somewhere between a 13 and a half and a fourteen when measured on a Brannock device.

Size, of course, depended on the brand. Anyone knew that.

These alligators were identical to a more costly pair of Stacy Adams Jimmy Frank had seen.

Good for nightlife.

Herm would discount them for Jimmy Frank.

It was hard enough for Jimmy Frank to find good fitting shoes in his size.

He was glad he didn't suffer from bunions or a hammertoe. This woman sounded like she lived in pure misery. Jimmy Frank flipped one of the alligators. The shoes were nice.

The problem was the extra height in the heel. Jimmy Frank was tall already. He didn't need the mobility issues these shoes would create. When you had to move, you didn't want an inch and a half of platform heel impeding your progress.

The woman started to moan when Herm brought out a third pair.

There was nothing practical or of orthopedic value with these shoes.

"They're so *pretty*," she said. She pointed at the shoes Herm brought to her. "But they would kill me dead."

"This pair's gonna look nice," Herm said.

Jimmy Frank smiled and nodded. Turned out Herman knew what he was doing.

The woman was practically stroking the pumps. Herm signaled. Give him five minutes.

❋ ❋ ❋

The men stood in the alley behind the shoe store.

Herm looking at Jimmy Frank like he was crazy.

"You wanna take on the Johnson brothers?" Herm said. "Gimme some of that reefer you smoking because you *must* be high, Jimmy Frank."

Jimmy Frank shook his head.

"Question is," he said. "Can you help a brother?"

"I can tell you tomorrow when they drop their money," Herm said. "Won't do any good less you can open their safe."

"You told me you knew a man could do that."

"I said that?" Herm said.

Jimmy Frank nodded his head.

"Damn," Herm said. "I wasn't thinking you were going after the Johnson brothers. That's bold, Jimmy Frank. You know what they would do if they find out it's you?"

"What's the man's name, Herm?"

You wanna open a safe, Phil Fontana is the man," Herm Taylor said. "Crazy Phil. Bratenahl Deluxe Autos."

Jimmy Frank shook his head.

"Unh-uh," Jimmy Frank said. "I won't work with

a man named Crazy."

Herm looked at Jimmy Frank. Pointed at him with the tip of his cigarette.

"Fontana's the best box-man in town. He's a pro. Open any kind of safe you got."

Jimmy Frank didn't say anything.

Herm looked at Jimmy Frank.

"You're for real, Jimmy Frank?"

Jimmy Frank nodded his head.

"Never been more real. This is a personal thing."

"I want in, Jimmy Frank," Herm Taylor said.

"I end up working with this Phil, there's no room. This is just a two man job, Herman," Jimmy Frank said.

"Can't do it with just two," Herm said. "You know the layout? You ever been in their place?"

"I been downstairs."

"They got a safe, but do you know where it is?" Herm said. "You know their wiring?"

"I can find out," Jimmy Frank said. "Figure this man Fontana knows his business."

Herm poked Jimmy Frank in the chest.

"Still and all this is at least a three man job. You need me, Jimmy Frank."

CALL ME

Eggy was drinking an Old Fashioned at his table at Eddie Swanson's Forest City.

The fill-in bartender served the drink just the way Eggy liked it.

Extra sugar, orange twist *and* a maraschino cherry.

Vic Collister wasn't sure how Eggy managed to slide up to the piano, but Eggy always ended up practically at Vic's elbow.

The place was about half full, but it was early in the evening.

"Vic," Eggy said. "I got a problem."

Vic nodded.

Part of Vic's skill as a piano player was his ability to carry on a conversation while playing cocktail music.

"What kinda problem you got, Egg?" Eggy didn't mind Vic calling him Egg. Maybe he liked the way it sounded better than Eggy.

"Diamond problems. They're serious," Eggy said.

Vic played a couple bars from *Diamonds are Forever*.

He entertained a quick thought of Jill St. John.

"Whattya mean, diamonds, Eggy?"

Eggy shook his head.

"I'm serious, Vic," he said. "This is a big, big, problem. I need your help. I know you know about this kinda thing. You got all your contacts. You know the score."

Eggy still had Vic pegged as an underworld confidant.

Vic shook his head.

"I dunno, Eggy," he said. "What I know about diamonds is pretty limited."

"Yeah," Eggy said. "But I just need to talk to somebody about this. Somebody with contacts."

Eggy leaned in. Gave a meaningful look.

"You know what I mean, Vic," he said. "Somebody with *contacts*."

"Give me the fake book version, Eggy," Vic said. "What's going on?"

"I can't tell you the whole story here," Eggy said. "Too many ears around here. I stay at the Alhambra, you know where that is?"

"The Alhambra?" Vic said. Smiled.

Vic knew the Alhambra like a book.

From the Art Deco lobby to the antique elevator leading to the pocket-sized ballroom.

He played in a society combo every once in a while.

Drums, bass, a sax, and Vic providing foxtrots, waltzes and the occasional cha-cha-cha for a pre-cotillion dancing school held in the fourth floor ballroom of the creaking Alhambra.

"Yeah," Vic said. "I know the Alhambra."

"Give me a call, okay?" Eggy said.

Eggy slid a card onto the lacquered piano near the bottom of the eighty-eight keys.

The Alhambra

Luxury Living

Timeless Atmosphere

Vic smiled. Timeless atmosphere. That was putting it mildly.

The place was old as the hills and it showed.

Vic brought his microphone in a little closer.

"And now a little new wave for you hepcats to dig," Vic said.

Played Blondie.

Call Me.

Eggy's brow's knitted. He was concentrating. An unusual look for Eggy.

Maybe he didn't know the song.

Vic tried a Petula Clark song.

Same title.

Call Me.

Eggy lit up. This one he knew.

"You can help me, I know it," he said. "Don't let me down, okay, Vic. I got a problem and it could get worse."

Vic shook his head no.

"I'm not your guy, Eggy," he said.

Eggy looked crestfallen.

"What are you talking about, Vic," he said. "You know everybody. You got contacts."

"I got a friend who's good at this stuff, Eggy," Vic said. "I'll give him a call."

"I don't know, Vic," Eggy said. "If he's a detective or something, he could get expensive. I'm not worried about myself, I'm worried about Natasha and her uncle. I think they got swindled."

Natasha and her uncle.

"Hal's your guy, Eggy," he said. "Hal Bailey. I'll call him."

Eggy looked at Vic.

"You think this guy is up for something like this?" Eggy said.

Vic looked at Eggy.

"Hal's good," Vic said. "I'd say he's just about perfect for you, Eggy. I'll call him when I go on break. Hal can help you."

THE ALHAMBRA

Hal Bailey threw his cigarette into the snow and walked up the steps to the Alhambra.

The phone booth in the lobby of the Alhambra was antique, just like the rest of the hotel.

Hal looked past the reception desk and up the sweeping staircase.

He almost expected to see Norma Desmond descending.

All right, Mr. DeMille. I'm ready for my close-up.

Gloria Swanson *had* stayed here in the thirties.

Cole Porter once tap danced on the grand piano in the bar. Celebrating *Night and Day*.

Now a guy named Williston "Eggy" Eglington III lived here.

Eggy.

Vic Collister had told Hal all about Eggy. Told him about the trust fund, the Old Fashioneds, the Dinty Moore. The whole miserable story about the diamonds.

"He's a patsy," Vic said, "but he's harmless. He doesn't need to get taken like this."

"Yeah, uh-huh," Hal said. "I'll see what I can do."

Hal dropped a dime in the glass-encased lobby phone. Called the front desk and asked for Eggy's room. He could have called from home, but from the way Vic Collister had described this guy, Hal didn't want to give Eggy extra time. Sometimes guys get in the middle of a funny situation like Eggy's, they take off.

Eggy answered on the seventh ring.

"Hope I didn't wake you up, Eggy," Hal said. "Vic Collister told me you needed some help."

"Hal Bailey, right?" Eggy said. "You're the guy Vic told me about. Boy am I glad you called."

"That's me," Hal said. "I'm down in the lobby. I can get a table."

"Give me ten minutes," Eggy said. "Order me a Bloody Mary. Tell them it's on my tab."

❊ ❊ ❊

Bailey looked around.

The waiter nodded when Bailey ordered coffee and told him Mr. Eglington would be joining them. Bailey balked at ordering Eggy the Bloody Mary. No reason to let their relationship get off to a start like that this early in the morning.

Two elderly women sat at separate tables across the room from Bailey. Kvetching about the weather. The snow didn't suit them.

"I just wish it would make up its mind," one woman said, "first it's snowing, then it's windy with ice."

"I could have been in Florida by now," the other woman said. "I should have been, but for the kids.

And it's once a year I need to make the great appearance. And for what? The granddaughter dresses like a barmaid and the grandson looks and talks like a pirate."

The first woman nodded her head.

"Yours too?" she said. "It's only getting worse."

* * *

At the breakfast table, Eggy looked over his shoulder and around the room.

Nobody was looking. The women were still yakking to each other and weren't paying attention to Eggy and Hal.

Hal looked at Eggy, who was dressed in a lime green jacket with a yellow shirt and an ascot.

Vic Collister hadn't exaggerated his description.

"Take a look at these," Eggy said.

He took a black velvet bag from the inside pocket of the jacket. After looking over his shoulder again, Eggy loosened the bag's drawstring and emptied three diamonds onto the white linen tablecloth.

Eggy motioned toward Hal.

"Take a close look at these babies," Eggy said. "Tell me what you think."

Hal shrugged. Looked at Eggy.

Besides Thurson Howell, who the hell wore ascots?

"I don't know diamonds. What do you want me to say about them?"

"You don't have to know anything about diamonds," Eggy said, "just look at them. What do you see?"

The diamonds glittered, even in the dim light of the Alhambra breakfast room.

"They look big," Hal said. "Big, valuable."

"Yeah, they are big," Eggy said. "You're right on the money there. That's where it ends."

"They aren't valuable?" Hal said. "Are they fake?"

Eggy nodded his head.

"I should start by telling you about my lady friend. She's an acquaintance, more or less. Not boyfriend-girlfriend yet, although I'm open to that. This lady I'm talking about? She's of Russian extraction. A very, very prominent family under Czar Nicholas. Her name is Natasha. Tell you the truth, I can't pronounce her last name even though she must have told me how a hundred times."

"These are her diamonds?" Hal said. "She got fake diamonds."

Eggy grimaced. He put his hands forward. Palms down. Silently quieting Hal.

"It's not so simple," Eggy said. "An uncle of hers just came out from the Soviet Union. Real hush-hush stuff, Natasha says. State department won't admit he's here officially lest the KGB gets wind. It's as scary as that. But he's here, all right. The uncle brought the diamonds." Eggy pointed at the diamonds in front of him. "He's got these big showy ones and then he's got industrial grade."

"But you said these were fake."

"I'm getting to that part," Eggy said.

"Okay," Hal said, "I just wanted to clarify the

situation."

"So Natasha," Eggy said. "She's a sweetheart, by the way. And smart? She's got an IQ off the chart. Very Russian. Plays chess. She's a Grand Master. They want her to teach math at a couple of colleges, but she's worried about the rest of her family. On account of the KGB. They're ruthless. They find out where the uncle is, you might as well hang it up. So Natasha comes to me. She just wanted to see if I could help. She was at the end of her rope. She didn't know who else to turn to."

"You two must get along," Hal said.

"We do," Eggy said. Hal thought he saw Eggy blush. He was smitten by the chess genius.

"She wanted to know if I wanted to buy a couple of the diamonds from her uncle," Eggy said. "She said it almost apologetically. She'd gone up to my apartment and made dinner for me. Which was nice, by the way. Heavy on red cabbage, but nice. She said the diamonds were a kind of a I'll-scratch-your-back-if-you-scratch-mine kind of deal. She said her uncle needed some cash, but he could get more diamonds later and I could make some money. His name's Sergei, by the way. This is the one who got out from behind the Iron Curtain. Anyway. Everything so far was on the up and up."

Hal looked at the diamonds.

They were big and shiny. They reminded him of a magazine ad for Keepsake Rings.

A dewy-eyed couple walking hand in hand down some path out in the country.

When you know it's for keeps.

He thought about Angie Mandarich.

Hal shook his head. His evening with Angie had gone just fine, but there was no reason to start thinking about wedding bells and diamond rings yet, if ever.

"So anyway," Eggy said. He cleared his throat.

"Sorry," Hal said. "I was a little lost there."

"No problem," Eggy said, "I'll try breaking the story down slow. Me and Natasha, the two of us, went up to a diamond brokerage up on the fourth floor of a place on St. Clair. Little office, but real busy. We met the uncle up there. We talked to a certified diamond appraiser. Sergei is getting kinda nervous about the broker seeing him. He was wondering if he should have worn a disguise. I guess it's a pretty competitive business. Cutthroat the way I understand it. Well, I understand his concern, cause you got to understand the uncle just escaped with these diamonds and the clothes on his back according to Natasha."

"The uncle," Hal said. "He's the one escaped with the diamonds, but he's worried the appraiser will recognize him?"

"I know," Eggy said, "but, see, if the wrong person in the diamond trade finds out who he is, all they got to do is tip off the KGB. They get a bounty and the uncle is pretty much dead. There are some baddies in diamonds. I'm telling you Hal, this is scary stuff. I know I can trust you, since you're friends with Vic, right?"

"Yeah," Hal said, "Vic and I go way back."

Hal used the end of his spoon to nudge one of the diamonds.

Eggy nodded at the diamond.

"Hardest element in the world," Eggy said. "That's why they use them for drill bits and so on. Not these, but the little ones. Kinda funny thinking these hunks of carbon will be here long after us, right? That's kinda funny."

Hal picked up one of the diamonds. Held it up to the light and stared at the facets. The diamonds were showy, anyway.

"I guess I never thought about that," Hal said.

"Me neither until all this," Eggy said, "Anyway, the appraiser looks at the diamonds and you shoulda seen his jaw drop. I mean he was amazed. Did I tell you about how he's got all these certificates behind him? Certified Gemologist. Diamond Ambassador. All that kind of jazz."

Hal nodded. He put the diamond down next to the other two.

"Pretty nice, huh?" Eggy said. "This guy's never seen clarity, purity, like the ones on the diamonds we showed him. And this is not a young guy. He's about as old as Natasha's uncle. It's like the appraiser's looking at the Mona Lisa of diamonds. I'm feeling a little bad at this point because I know I'm gonna make a killing if I buy them. I'm wondering if I'm taking advantage of the old man who just got to this country. I said something like that to Natasha and she told me not to worry about it. Her uncle just wants to make sure I know the diamonds are good. That's why we're getting them checked out. Plus, she says we can get more later. Same size, same quality. Just as soon as her uncle's brother gets out of the Soviet Union, too."

"Wouldn't that be her uncle too?" Hal said. "I mean the uncle's brother."

Eggy looked at Hal. Nodded his head.

"Technically, I guess you're right," he said.

"Don't let me interrupt," Hal said.

Eggy continued.

"So, I figure I'll buy these for myself, and I ask Natasha if she wants me to buy some for her. Just for an investment. See, I like Natasha. Not like boyfriend-girlfriend, like I said. At least not yet, but I'd be happy to help her out."

Hal nodded.

"Just help her out."

"Right," Eggy said. "I'm like that."

"Did you know the diamond appraiser or did Natasha and her uncle set this up?" Hal said.

"The guy worked for the brokerage," Eggy said. "Natasha contacted him. He was able to fit us in and that wasn't easy to do before Christmas. Plus, the whole diamond world is a very close-knit community I found out. Everybody knows everybody. Anyway, what difference does it make who contacted who?"

Hal shook his head. Looked over at the ladies at the other table.

"Oh, I don't know," Hal said. "I just figured I

should ask."

Eggy scooped the diamonds into the bag. Looked over Hal's shoulder.

The waiter arrived carrying a tray.

He placed an order of eggs Benedict in front of Eggy.

Eggy tucked a white napkin into his collar. Held up a fork.

"Sure you don't want some of these eggs?" he said. "They make them good here. Benedict or Florentine. On me."

Hal shook his head.

"So what's the problem, Eggy? Why did Vic call me? He said you had a problem."

Eggy chewed a piece of English muffin with Hollandaise sauce. Pointed at the black bag.

"So I bought them. I also bought two for Natasha."

Hal nodded.

"Just on a lark, I'm thinking about getting them set into jewelry. Couple cufflinks, I'm thinking even though I can count on one hand how many black ties I go to in a year nowadays. Things aren't the same as they used to be. I ask Natasha if she wants to go with me to the jeweler, maybe look over a couple things, just for fun. I'm thinking maybe she'd go for some kind of brooch. She's a spectacular looking woman. Very Slavic, I don't know if I mentioned. Think Gina Lollobrigida, but think Slavic at the same time. Turns out she couldn't go."

"So what happened then?"

"Well, that's the thing," Eggy said. "A couple days later, I take them to this jeweler I know. Figure he could get the stones into some nice settings. And this guy, he takes them and looks them over and then he calls out another guy out of the back. Both of them start laughing. Asks me how much I paid for them. He tells me these diamonds are fake. Well, not exactly fake. He says they're *cubic zirconium*. Ever heard of something like that?"

Hal shook his head.

"Nope," he said. "Never. What do you call them again?"

"*Cubic Zirconium*. It comes out of the Soviet Union. They are some kind of industrial diamonds. Synthetic," Eggy said. "Soviet Union stands to reason, I guess. But when I go back to the place on St. Clair, the jewelry brokerage is gone. I told Natasha about all this and she flips out. First of all, she can't believe the diamonds are fake. And until I got her calmed down she was a little angry with me for taking them to another jeweler. She said it sounded like I didn't trust her. And that's as far from the truth as you can get, Hal. I swear. I trust Natasha. She's honest. But that was only the first thing."

"What was the second thing?" Hal said. Leaning forward.

"She and her uncle have got a real problem now," Eggy said. "It's not just those diamonds."

"Not just the diamonds?" Hal said.

"Exactly," Eggy said. "Natasha started crying and she just can't stop. Turns out the broker was keeping all the uncle's diamonds for him. You know, they said they had a safe and they were going to keep them for the uncle. I mean, here he is walking around with a million dollars worth of diamonds. That's when I figure the whole thing out. And what I need is your help."

"What did you figure out?"

"I figured out the guy on St. Clair traded the diamonds I bought for the phony ones. I don't know how he did it. Some kind of switcheroo. Then, when the old man trusted them with his whole stash he realized he was sitting on a fortune. The temptation was too much for the guy. So he took off with the old man's diamonds."

"Uh huh," Hal said, "that's what you figured out?"

"I mean, what else could it be?" Eggy said. "Now I can't get in touch with the old man."

Hal nodded.

"And I'm worried about Natasha. She's not answering my phone calls."

"This place you're talking about. On St. Clair. You still got the address?"

Eggy shook his head yes.

"It looks like a ghost town, now. Before, there were people in there, buying, selling, I don't know what else."

"How much are you out?" Hal said.

"Money-wise?" Eggy said.

"Yeah, money-wise. How much did you give the old man?"

"He gave me a deal on account of me being good to Natasha. He said they were worth thirty grand easy. So did the appraiser. He took five grand for all of them. So I got what? A twenty-five thousand dollar discount for cash. I wouldn't have insisted on that much. You know what the thing is?"

Hal shook his head.

"I'm worried about Natasha. I figure the old man can take care of himself. I'm just worried about her and what she must be going through."

"You think she's going through something?" Hal said.

Eggy looked at Hal.

"What do you think? Jeez. It's her uncle. She's worried sick about the old guy. He's new in this country. He doesn't exactly have the right paperwork. He could get himself in trouble. Maybe deported."

"So what did she say?" Hal said.

"Natasha?" Eggy said. He pushed his hands in front of him. Palms up.

He hadn't touched the eggs.

"Last thing she said was she was going to find those guys from up on St. Clair if it's the last thing she ever does," Eggy said. "She was pretty worked up. She was talking really fast with an accent. I didn't understand half what she was saying over the phone."

"When was this?" Hal said.

"This was when I called her. Few days ago. Four days? Five?"

Eggy shook his head.

"Now I can't find her. It's like she's dropped off the face of the earth."

"Yeah," Hal said, "unfortunately, that may just be the way it goes."

Eggy looked at him.

"You mean it?" he said.

Hal nodded.

Eggy screwed up his face.

"But Vic said you could help. That's why I asked him to get in touch with you."

Hal looked at Eggy.

"I'll tell you what," Hal said. "I can't promise anything, but I'll see if I can find Natasha. I take a daily fee and I charge expenses."

"I can write a post-dated check for the first of next month," Eggy said. "If that's okay."

Hal remembered the arrangement of Eggy's trust money.

"That's fine, Eggy," Hal said. "Make it out to Hal Bailey. Nothing else, if you don't mind. Matter of fact, if I bring it back to you and you change it for cash, I'll give you a discount."

The promise of a new day brightened Eggy's face.

"That's fine," Eggy said. " I just want to know Natasha is okay. I don't care about the money."

Yeah, nobody ever cares about the money, right?

"That's good," Hal said. "I'm pretty sure you

won't see the five grand again."

"You're not sure?" Eggy said.

Crestfallen.

"Look," he said, "I just want to help Natasha and her uncle. Plus, when the other uncle comes over, I could make a little money out of the deal. I wouldn't mind that. One hand washes the other."

Hal thought about the situation.

"I'll take Natasha's address if you've got it," he said.

"I just have where she works," Eggy said. Brightening.

"Great," Hal said.

"The Samovar," Eggy said. "It's a place on Coventry next to a dance studio. You know where that is?"

"I'll find it," Hal said.

It wasn't every day you get to talk to a Slavic Lollobrigida.

BOOKS BY STANISLAVSKI

"This is good," Stan said.

Hal and Stan were sitting at the Swabian Club. Stan had just come in, put his coat, hat, scarf in the booth and sat across from Hal.

"Glad you called," Stan said, "Good chance to get to know you. Angie's always talking about you."

"Your name's Stanislaus or plain Stanley?" Hal said. "I'm curious."

"Stanislaus," Stan said. "I was named for the saint. Patron saint of Poland."

"Okay," Hal said. "I just wondered. I wonder if Mitch Walczak knows that."

Stan looked at him. Laughed.

"Your friend's name is Walczak, believe me, he knows Saint Stan."

When the waiter came to their table, Stan ordered the kielbasa and pierogi plate. Hal was still looking the menu over. Leaning toward spätzli. It was good at the Swabian Club. Not too heavy.

"Just a sec," Hal said, "Short notice, I know, but I wanted to talk something over with you."

"You can't beat the kielbasa here," Stan said. "Even though this place isn't Polish.

Hal shook his head. Kept looking at the menu.

Along with spätzli, Hal would have liked liver and onions the way they served them here at the Swabian Club. Surprisingly, Hal had never found liver served anywhere nearly as good as at the Swabian. Maybe someday he would have liver and onions with the spätzli on the side.

"You need more time?" the waiter said.

"No," Hal said. "I'll get the kielbasa and pierogi like my friend here."

Stan nodded. Approvingly.

"Angie's talked about you. She says you're a good guy. She meets a lot of guys cutting hair like she does, me and my brother Ted sometimes worry. You know, about creeps."

He looked at Hal.

On the other hand, having the liver and onions *and* the spätzli might be too heavy. Ordering both was something Mitch Walczak would do.

Hal nodded.

"It's a good thing you and your brother keep your eye on Angie," he said.

"You know what?" Stan said, "We don't have to worry about her. She's got a good head on her shoulders. She's not going to have anything to do with a problem guy."

"Stan," Hal said, "I wanted to ask you something. I wanted to see if you could do me a favor. A little acting, kinda. Angie said you act."

"Just little theater stuff," Stan said. "It's just for fun for now."

"You ever studied acting?" Hal said.

Stan nodded. Got a serious look on his face. Brow furrowed.

"I got a couple books by Stanislavski," Stan said. "They're pretty deep. Deeper than I need, maybe. Mostly I just been learning as I go along."

"You get paid sometimes, like in the little theater productions?"

Stan shook his head no.

"I wish," he said. "Maybe I will sometime. Angie said I should get some head shots made go for some commercials. I'm thinking more like I could be a kind of ethnic Claude Akins. You ever watch *Movin' On* on TV?"

"Love it," Hal said. "It's one of my favorites. Waylon singing that song?"

"Yeah," Stan said. "That's the one. Akins did pretty good with that."

"My thing's kinda for fun, too," Hal said. "But I *can* give you a couple bucks, just to make it interesting."

DARLING BE HOME SOON

Jackie parked under Chief Wahoo at Cleveland Municipal Stadium as he'd been directed.

Late afternoon but already getting dark. Jackie was waiting for Phil Fontana to show up. He was trying to stay warm. The heater in the Chevy Monza could have been a little stronger, but Jackie was okay in the down jacket he wore.

Chief Wahoo towered over Lake Erie. Thirty feet of sheet metal and neon.

There were no other cars near the stadium.

Jackie played with the radio.

Darling be Home Soon by the Lovin' Spoonful.

Jackie raised and lowered the volume on the stereo.

Go...

And beat your crazy head against the sky.

Try...

The Monza had been left at Easy Al's. Chances were good the car was abandoned. That happened sometimes, Conn said. People left cars and never picked them up. Despite some rust, the car had pep. The Monza had been at Easy Al's so long Jackie felt like he owned the car.

Jackie knew how to change an odometer. The procedure was no more difficult than setting the calendar on a Timex watch.

Jackie changed the mileage periodically in case the owner did show up.

Phil Fontana was late now. Jackie was getting fidgety. Smoke hung in the front seat of the Monza from the Marlboros Jackie chain smoked.

My darling be home sooooon.

Jackie hated cracking the side-vent of the Monza. You never knew if the window would close again. But the smoke was heavy.

He pulled another crumpled Marlboro from his shirt.

Jackie had just turned twenty-seven years old a couple months before.

He was thinking about his age and what he'd done with his life so far which was not much.

He could make some easy money doing a few jobs for Phil Fontana.

Get away from Cleveland. Go somewhere nice.

He pictured himself on a beach or a tropical island.

Jackie shook his head.

Twenty-seven years old. By this age, Jim Morrison was already dead.

Pthwmk. The lighter ejected. Jackie looked at the blaze-orange ring, held it next to his cigarette.

Some guys Jackie knew had been at the steel mill

for a couple years. Union jobs. Making good money. Married, living in real houses. Not in tiny studio apartments like where Jackie lived.

He had moved out of his family's house after high school.

He said he liked his freedom. Nobody told Jackie what he needed to do anymore.

Before working at the parking lot, Jackie sold records at a place on Coventry.

Jackie sold pot at the record store under the table. After a while, Jackie quit the record shop and tried just selling pot.

That didn't last long either. Jackie got too nervous worrying which one of the pukes he sold the dime bags to was an undercover narcotics officer. It was just a matter of time before he got nailed. Jackie didn't want to go to prison for any reason, but he especially didn't want to go for something stupid. What could be stupider than that?

Then he'd gone to work at Easy Al's.

He was good at the job. Conn Rutherford said Jackie was a natural. Conn wasn't the kind of guy who just handed out complements.

There was a sign in big letters on the brick wall of the building next to the lot:

Let Easy Al Park You

But it wasn't Al and it wasn't Conn who did the parking. It was Jackie.

Even though it was cold as hell in the winter, Jackie liked working at Easy Al's.

Jackie made good money at Easy Al's.

Jackie could move a car in and out of the lot as fast and accurate as you'd ever seen.

Conn said the only way to make money was to pack the lot tight as sardines.

Open space in the lot meant less money.

The name of the game was volume, Conn said.

Most people paid with cash.

* * *

Jackie heard a knock on the window. He put his cigarette into the ashtray and looked out.

Phil Fontana stood next to the Monza wearing the same get-up he wore earlier.

Same winter-weight London Fog overcoat. Same trilby hat. Same grouse feather. The briar pipe between his teeth made a gurgling noise when Fontana inhaled.

Everything about Fontana said *square* to Jackie.

* * *

Phil drove to the stadium in the brown Dodge Challenger then directed Jackie to take the wheel.

There was another man in the back seat of the Challenger.

Phil Fontana pointed at the guy who was hunched into a ball.

The guy worked his way up like a rusty jack-in-the-box. He wore a blue windbreaker and a flat tartan cap. A cigarette was tucked behind the guy's ear.

"That's Jerry in the back seat," Fontana said. "He's going with us. I wanted you two to get to know each other."

Jerry nodded toward Jackie.

"Jackie, Jerry," Fontana said. "Jerry, Jackie."

"Jerry Lalonde," the guy said. "It's a French name. Accent on the last syllable. Matter of fact, there should be an accent and an internal capital L. A lotta people get that wrong."

"Jerry doesn't talk much," Fontana said. "But he's a helluva talented guy."

"You got a lotta Lalondes in Quebec up there," Jerry said. "It's part of my family. Newsy Lalonde played hockey for the Canadiens back in what? In the teens? Twenties? I'm distantly related to Newsy on my father's side. My mother's people were from Ireland."

Fontana leaned over the seat.

"That's great, Jerry," he said. "You just let me do the talking from here, okay?"

"Perfectly okay, Phil," Jerry said. "Just wanted to let this kid know my *bona fides*, if that's okay with you, Phil. You know, in case we're working together like you said."

Jackie looked back at Jerry. The guy had pulled a toothpick from his shirt pocket and was giving his back teeth a going over.

This was Fontana's team of experts?

Jackie took Fontana and Jerry on a ride. They drove from the stadium past the Terminal Tower then down Euclid Avenue.

"Don't ask me what's under the hood, Jackie," Fontana said. "The nitrous is legal but the rest of it ain't."

Jackie made the car hug the road like one of Fontana's pigskin gloves. Jackie ran the car fast, but not too fast. Peeled out a couple of times. Did some quick turnarounds. Showy stuff for Fontana's benefit. Jackie knew what he was doing with a car. He liked showing his stuff.

"You got the *Dukes of Hazzard* thing down pretty good," Fontana said.

Jackie Dunne ignored Fontana.

Jackie modeled his driving after Steve McQueen. *LeMans*, baby.

Jackie let his driving do the talking.

Fontana had Jackie pull over at Hough Bakery.

"Do me a favor," Fontana said.

He scooped a couple of dollars out of his pocket.

"Run in and get a couple jelly doughnuts, wouldja?"

"Doughnuts?" Jackie said. "You're kidding me, right?"

"I got a thing about 'em," Fontana said. "It's a weakness, I'll admit it. I can't have more than a couple a day on account of my waistline. Go ahead and grab one for yourself you like. Get the day-old ones, though. They're just as good."

Fontana leaned over the seat.

"Hey Jerry," he said. "Ya wanna doughnut?"

Jerry Lalonde looked up. Squinted. Rubbed his stomach.

"Normally yes, but right now? No-can-do," he said. "Thanks for the offer, I don't wanna ruin my appetite. The old lady would have my ass."

Jackie went in and bought the doughnuts, but he didn't get one for himself. Even the jelly doughnuts were covered with powdered sugar. Jackie didn't want to get the wheel sticky.

When Jackie came out of Hough Bakery, both Jerry Lalonde and Phil Fontana were on the curb next to the Challenger.

"Watch this, Jackie," Fontana said. "This thing you will not believe. Do you have the keys to the car?"

Of course Jackie didn't have the keys. He'd left the car running when he went in to get the doughnuts.

He shook his head.

"Check the doors," Fontana said. "Make sure they're locked."

All the doors were locked. Jackie double-checked them.

"What are you getting at, Phil?" Jackie said.

Fontana laughed.

He pulled the Challenger's keys from his pocket, dangling them for a second before dropping them back into his pocket.

"Just watch this," Fontana said. "This you won't believe."

Fontana turned, looked at his watch. Spoke to Jerry Lalonde.

"All right, Jerry," he said. "I got my watch set. Ready, go."

Jerry walked toward the Challenger, pulling something which looked like a retractable ruler out of his pocket.

In less than a minute, he was in the car. His head, flat hat, cigarette, and all, had ducked beneath the steering wheel.

A few seconds later, Dodge's engine came to life.

"One minute and forty-seven seconds," Fontana said. "That's about par for Jerry."

Jerry Lalonde opened the drivers side door and hopped out.

"Sorry it took so long," he said. "Wires on the back side got a little fussy."

"You did fine," Fontana said. "Jackie, you get back in the driver's seat. You're still driving."

"Listen," Jerry Lalonde said, "this is all fine and dandy, but I gotta get home. No fooling."

Jackie and Fontana left Jerry Lalonde at his house. Jerry's wife was looking through the curtains.

"Aw jeez," Jerry said. "Am I in trouble now, or what? Listen, just call me when you need me. Far as I'm concerned, everything's copacetic."

❉ ❉ ❉

"I don't know why Jerry was so chatty tonight,"

Fontana said. "Normally you can't get two words out of the guy. He musta been a little nervous, I don't know. Anyway, he was impressed with your driving. He said so when you were getting the doughnuts."

Jackie nodded. He didn't feel good about working with Jerry Lalonde.

"One more stop, Jackie," Fontana said.

"Make a turn here," Fontana said. "You see the sign says Bratenahl Deluxe? That's my place. Let's stop here for a minute.

Inside Bratenahl Deluxe Motors, Fontana locked the door. Rolled down the shades.

"Sometimes I gotta get a car back from somebody buys it," Fontana said.

Jackie nodded.

"Like not just my cars, other cars," Fontana said. "Sometimes some very nice ones. High end."

"Stolen?" Jackie said.

"Whoa," Fontana said. "That's a big jump right there."

"Okay," Jackie said, "where do I come in?"

"You just drive," Fontana said. "I thought we established that. Jerry's the one who performs the magic."

He looked at Jackie again.

"You're wondering how much money is involved? You won't walk away with less than two bills. For driving."

"Two hundred," Jackie said. "For driving."

Fontana took off his hat and scratched his head.

Looked at Jackie.

"You make that much parking cars?"

Jackie shook his head.

"So far so good?"

"You're knocking something over," Jackie said, "I'm not gonna do anything like that."

Phil held up both hands like a stop sign.

"Whoa, whoa, whoa. You're imagining things, Jackie."

Fontana grinned.

"All you do is drive. You just saw how Jerry does his thing. Only thing is, I need a driver, on account of Jerry is perhaps the worst driver in the world. No kidding, he'll admit it. Man can't drive. So, after he gets the car started, you take it away. He leaves in the clunker we send you out in. If needed, Jerry can create a diversion. Like he can sideswipe another car if he has to. I got a lawyer can get either of you out of anything. I'll tell you more later. I'm just doing you a courtesy here. Letting you know what we're talking about."

"Okay," Jackie said. "That's good, because I'm not interested in knocking anyone over."

"Perfectly reasonable," Phil said.

"I just drive. I don't knock anybody over," Jackie said. "I'm no Charles Bronson. No death wish for me whatsoever."

Fontana shook his head no. Gave Jackie a nothing-could-be-further-from-my-intentions look.

"Who said anything about a death wish?

Nothing like that, Jackie. It's nothing like that."

Jackie looked out the window. It was completely dark.

"Listen, Jackie," Phil said. "Nobody's knocking anybody over. You just sit in the car staying warm. Just likes when you were waiting there under Chief Wahoo. That's all you got to do. Jerry does the work. He's a mechanical genius. He's specialized. Just like you are. I only hire specialists. You aren't knocking anyone over, you're just driving."

Jackie nodded. Pretending he understood Fontana.

He looked around the interior of Bratenahl Deluxe Motors.

Nothing about the place looked deluxe.

"Two hundred?" he said.

Fontana nodded.

"At the minimum," he said.

"You don't go along?" Jackie said.

Fontana shook his head.

"I'm a behind the scenes guy," he said. "I kinda produce and direct, you dig?"

Jackie nodded. There was more to the guy than he thought, but still, he wasn't sure he wanted to get involved with this kind of thing.

"You're not knocking anything over?"

"Cross my heart," Fontana said.

Jackie thought.

"Sometimes, I might send the two of you out of town," Fontana said. "Like, say I got somebody who needs a particular kind of car. High end. And I know how to get the car. With you two, I can make that happen."

"High end?" Jackie said.

"Cadillacs, Mercedes. Maybe a Lincoln. Something like that you get extra. Plus per diem."

Jackie shook his head.

Two hundred was a lot. It would come in handy. He had to park a lot of cars for that kind of money. And he would be doing something he could do better than anyone.

He shook his head.

"Yeah," Jackie said, "repo work is one thing. Stealing cars is another."

"Look," Fontana said, "that's just one way of describing it. A lotta people get themselves over their head in their car payments. They *want* out of the loan. It's a service. I gotta be up front. Jerry does like to bring along a gun. It's like when the president says *Trust but verify*. Guns convince. So, ideally, you never see any gun, but just in case."

Jackie didn't say anything.

Guns.

Driving around with Jerry Lalonde.

Fontana looked at Jackie Dunne.

Waiting.

"I gotta think about it," he said.

"That's your answer?" Phil said.

"That's it," Jackie said. "I gotta think about it."

Fontana looked at Jackie.

"You know no matter what you decide, you can't talk about this," Fontana said. "Needless to say."

Jackie nodded. Wishing he could just give the guy a flat no.

"I don't talk about stuff like that," he said.

Fontana didn't say anything for maybe a half a minute.

Just looked at Jackie.

"All right, then," he said. "Let's get you back to Chief Wahoo."

* * *

Jackie didn't know how Conn knew he'd been with Phil Fontana.

Jackie brought the Monza back to the parking lot from the stadium.

Conn was still at Easy Al's, even though the parking lot was closed.

Jackie didn't see Conn until he spoke.

"You gonna work for that guy?" Conn said.

Jackie looked surprised.

He looked at Conn.

"What guy are you talking about, Conn?"

Conn looked at Jackie.

"Who you think you're kidding, Jackie? I'm talking about the guy with the hat."

Jackie's expression was blank.

"Same guy came around the other day. I see him again today, talking with you, right? Guy with the corny hat. He asked about you. First thing, I thought he was a cop."

Jackie nodded.

"Then, I figured out the guy wasn't any cop."

Jackie nodded.

"I didn't say I was working for him, did I?"

The shack was dark except for the heater.

"You didn't say you weren't working for him, either."

The Stroh's was the last can in the bag. Conn wadded the brown paper and pried the top from the Strohs can.

"Doesn't matter what you say, Jackie. I know what a guy like him is all about. If you decide to work for him, just lemme give you a couple hints."

Conn sipped the Strohs. Looked out the window.

Jackie looked at Conn.

"I got no idea what you're talking about, Conn."

"I think you do, Jackie," Conn said. "Either way, though, it doesn't matter. You wanna work for him, talk to me first."

"I'll do that," Jackie said. Knowing he wouldn't

Conn nodded his head.

"Good," he said. "That's a good decision. You wanna be smart in life, Jackie."

JUST THE WAY YOU ARE

Hank Standish stood on the other side of the bar from Jimmy Frank Waters at Eddie Swanson's Forest City.

Jimmy Frank watched Hank.

The joint was busy tonight, both in the dining room and here in the bar.

Hank Standish had decided to try out his voice tonight.

Over Hank Standish's voice Jimmy Frank heard Vic Collister playing piano in the dining room.

Vic, was starting his Christmas shtick on the piano, teasing two or three bars of Mel Tormé.

The diners groaned but they loved it. It was all in good fun.

"Too early for some Jack Frost nipping?" Vic said.

Vic was a pro.

Sliding back into *Seventh Son,* you'd think Vic Collister was Mose Allison himself.

Uhn uhn uhn uhn uhn uhn UHN...

Everybody's talking 'bout the seventh son...

Jimmy Frank was still filling in for Herm Taylor.

Herm had commitments elsewhere this week and had called Jimmy Frank saying he still wouldn't make it in and would Jimmy Frank please, please cover one more night, please.

In the whole round world there is only one...

Jimmy Frank knew he didn't even need to listen to Hank Standish, still, the man was getting on his nerves.

Going on and on. Forgetting Jimmy Frank's name even though Jimmy Frank had been serving him all week.

Hank Standish had called him Herm instead of Jimmy Frank every night.

Other than that he'd been quiet until tonight.

Tonight Hank Standish was talking up a storm.

❊ ❊ ❊

Hank Standish was just this side of fifty.

Maybe younger, Jimmy Frank couldn't say. Gray clipped hair with the Grecian Formula look. Tattersall shirt open at the collar. Blue blazer. Sporty. Not much difference between Hank and any of the other men who came to Eddie Swanson's Forest City.

They all looked about the same to Jimmy Frank. They lined up at the bar, each grabbing a stiff one before getting on the Rapid and heading back to the east suburbs. Already dark in the late afternoon.

Not much difference except Hank Standish had

planted his flag at the bar the last couple of nights.

Hank Standish had been quiet until tonight.

Now, it turned out Hank Standish was a world-class talker. He went on and on and on.

And the man didn't care *who* was listening, apparently.

So far he'd announced that Hilda Standish, God bless her, was out of town. Hilda didn't like the winter and God knows who does. She left Cleveland and Hank in order to get down to Florida where she could soak up the sun and play tennis outside for crying out loud. Hank was batching it. Hilda had left a couple days after Thanksgiving leaving a stack of Stouffer's frozen dinners in the icebox and Hank at loose ends.

Blah, blah, blah.

In the dining room, Vic Collister played Billy Joel.

Just the Way You Are.

Don't go changing.

Just like that, Louise Atkinson came into the bar.

Try and please me.

Louise sat down next to Hank Standish.

Like on television. Mary Tyler Moore sitting down next to Ed Asner.

Louise put her pack of cigarettes on the bar. Waved hi to Jimmy Frank.

Jimmy Frank looked at Hank Standish. Jimmy Frank had Hank figured out now.

Hank wasn't *about* to get a table on account of there being too much chance of meeting people he knew in the dining room.

Talking about Hilda and Florida and the Stouffer's macaroni and beef dinners was okay in the bar, but not in the dining room.

There's a mile-long canyon worth of difference between drinking alone and eating alone.

＊ ＊ ＊

Hank Standish saw things were getting worse outside with the snow. Hell, it had been bad when he had come in, just to get a bracer, before getting on the Rapid.

The snow was falling sideways down Short Vincent Avenue outside the Forest City.

Who wants to brave the elements half-sober, even when all you had to do was get to the Terminal Tower and catch the goddamn Rapid?

Hank Standish didn't.

Herm Taylor wasn't tending bar tonight. He hadn't been there all week.

The fill-in was working.

Hank Standish couldn't remember the fill-in's name but the guy was generous with the bourbon so Hank had no problem with him.

The fill-in was a big tall guy with a semi-long Afro.

Maybe the guy could lose a couple of pounds but he might have been an athlete at one time. He looked like a linebacker. Hank himself had played a million years ago. The cold always reminded him of his days on the gridiron.

Hank turned.

A woman had come into the bar. She sat down next to Hank.

She sat so close to Hank he could smell her perfume. Not overpowering though. Nice. Subtle.

She looked familiar, but Hank couldn't place her. Was she the one who coached tennis at the club? Hilda loved *her*.

Maybe she was. Hank wasn't sure, though. He knew he'd seen her somewhere.

She placed a pack of Virginia Slims in front of her place at the bar.

There was a lot going on in what Hilda called *Hank's complicated mind*.

Hank and the woman started to chat a little.

Nothing much, just talking about the shitty weather.

It's gonna get worse I heard. Oh really? That kind of thing.

Her name was Louise.

He asked her name twice, subtly both times.

Hank stopped himself from saying, *God you don't look like any Louise I ever met*. Even though she didn't.

With Louise on the scene, things were looking up. Now Hank had somebody to talk to. Even though he knew he'd been talking all night.

She was listening to him.

This woman, did he know her? What was her name?

"Louise Atkinson," she said.

Louise might be thirty-five, thirty-six years old. She couldn't be any older than that.

Blonde hair. Blue eyes. Tan. Straight white teeth. Straight from the Florida Sunshine Tree, right?

Hank started telling Louise about a fancy doo-dad. A tiara.

This thing had been in the family for years. Hank wasn't sure why he'd even brought the topic up.

Well, she said she loved antiques and *objets d'art*, and Hank didn't mind blowing a little smoke with a pretty girl.

Now he was committed to the goddamn story.

Sometimes Hank got on tangents when he was tight. He would start talking about family lore and he didn't know when to stop.

"This tiara," Hank said. "Family legend says it belonged to Marie Antoinette."

God, what an old story, he thought. Just like a dopey game of show and tell.

But she was listening. Hanging on his words and looking at Hank with her blue eyes.

So he kept going.

"They set a place up for her in Pennsylvania," Hank said. "Marie Antoinette. You can look it up. Place is still there. She was supposed to go to Pennsylvania for crying-out-loud. Obviously *that* never panned out."

Hank's voice might have belonged to somebody else. He felt like he'd gone out of his body with the last drink. He knew he should stop talking, but he couldn't.

He didn't want to bore this woman.

Louise.

Eventually Hank knew he was going to start talking about Hilda and he didn't want to.

He would tell Louise all about Hilda.

How Hilda really was an exceptionally attractive woman.

Still exceptional, Hilda was.

Except Hilda was currently in Florida.

Hank was only talking about the tiara because Louise, that *was* her name, was interested.

"Something like this tiara. It's gotta be priceless, right?" he said to Louise. "I mean, this is just a rhetorical question, but can you even put a pricetag on it? Something, when you know it belongs, I mean, belonged to Marie Antoinette, it's gotta be worth a fortune, right? Priceless."

She had just walked into the bar. As far as Hank knew, Louise had never been here before.

Hank had never seen her before, and Hank never forgot a pretty face, did he?

"Gosh," Louise said, "Marie Antoinette? It must be amazing. I can only imagine."

Hank was about seven double bourbons deep and he wasn't slowing down.

Not that he kept score.

He'd taken a couple warm-up shots at the office before getting to Eddie's, but those didn't count.

Not on the nightly statistics anyway.

* * *

Hank Standish was talking to Louise Atkinson now.

Jimmy Frank poured Hank's bourbon with a loose hand. Jimmy Frank didn't care. It wasn't like the booze belonged to him.

Booze belonged to Eddie Swanson. Who knew if there even was an Eddie Swanson?

Dude could be like Santa Claus for all Jimmy Frank knew.

It was the holiday season after all, especially at Eddie Swanson's.

Jimmy Frank's feelings were now under control.

His attitude about Hank Standish was different. The tiara had gotten Jimmy Frank's attention.

Jimmy Frank didn't mind listening to whatever Hank wanted to say about the tiara.

Marie Goddam Antoinette.

Jimmy Frank watched the man waving his arms, trying to impress Louise.

Hank Standish didn't know who he was talking to.

"It was my mother's," Hank Standish said. "This thing, the tiara, it looks like Wedgwood. Jasperware, right? I mean *get-out-of-here,* right? The damn tiara's coated in porcelain. Only way you know something's inside it is if you shake it, which my mother warned us not to do by the way. But when you take a look at the bottom, the inscription tells the story. Plain English. You don't even have to speak French."

Hank Standish was talking to Louise Atkinson

and giving her the eye at the same time.

"Goes back two hundred years. Marie Antoinette and her son were gonna settle in Pennsylvania. I'll bet you didn't know *that* little tidbit. This, after hubby went to the guillotine. Louis the what? Seventeen. I'm kind of an expert. Look it up you don't believe me. Smithsonian wants it. They would *love* to have it. They would give their collective eyeteeth to have it."

Waving his arm in the direction of Washington D.C.

"I've gotten *umpteen* letters from them. And you know what I say to them? You know what I say to the whole goddam Smithsonian Institute?"

Jimmy Frank could see Hank liked Louise.

Why wouldn't he? She was easy to talk to.

"The Wedgwood tiara," Louise said. "Sounds like a Perry Mason story."

Hank Standish looked at her. Laughed.

"You're right," he said. "That's a good one, Louise."

She smiled. He'd gotten her name right.

He smiled back at her. Picked up a cigarette. Lighted the wrong end.

* * *

Louise ordered a rum and coke when she came in the bar.

Light on the rum.

Jimmy Frank put the drink in front of her.

Raised his eyebrows. Gave her a look.

The guy next to her was talking and talking.

Louise had finished a long day at the flower shop.

Somebody died and the shop got hit with last minute orders.

"This is nothing," Larry Carmichael said, you should see us when we get *busy*."

Larry was Louise's boss at the flower shop. Larry reminded Louise every so often he was *taking a chance* on her.

"This order? This is absolutely *nothing*. This kinda thing is what you gotta expect when you're doing a family funeral."

Larry raised his eyebrows when he said the word family.

"You mean like mafia?" Louise said.

"Don't say that word, Louise," Larry said. "I never want to hear you say that word again. God, put more baby's breath on that one. And don't let it wilt."

The guy at the bar kept talking.

Louise sipped her rum and coke. She told the man standing next to her at the bar she was here waiting for Vic Collister, the piano player.

Vic had waved at Louise from the piano when she went into the dining room. She'd gone up to Vic and he'd smiled at her, but there was something in the way he looked at her. No emotion. Nothing more than the superficial cocktail piano smile he gave all the time.

She wondered if she liked Vic more than he liked her. She wondered if he liked her at all.

"Meet me at Johnny's after?" he said.

They always met at Johnny's before going to her place. Never his.

What would he say if she said no?

"If you're lucky, she said."

"Get Jimmy Frank to set you up," Vic said.

* * *

This man was maybe twenty years older than Louise.

He was a little bit drunk.

He had already asked Louise her name twice.

Now he was telling her about his family's treasure. A ceramic covered tiara maybe belonged to Marie Antoinette.

It was a good story, anyway.

Louise had left her Volare parked down the street. The good-looking kid wedged her car into a back space at Easy Al's Parking.

Louise liked Eddie Swanson's, but she couldn't sit in the dining room watching people eat all night.

This was the time of night where Vic bounced between Union Gap songs and the Grass Roots.

Sooner or later love is gonna get ya.

Vic told Louise he didn't believe in challenging the musical tastes of the diners.

"I stay where the customer's heads are at," Vic said. "They want roast beef, red wine, middle-of-the-road music. Give 'em what they want, right?"

* * *

Hank Standish looked at her again. He swept his eyes from her knees to her head then back to her knees.

"You know what I would say to the whole goddam Smithsonian Institute?" Hank said.

"I can't imagine," Louise said.

Jimmy Frank leaned in.

He picked up a bar rag. Showing Louise and Hank he wasn't listening.

"I tell the whole goddam Smithsonian Institute where to stick it," Hank said. "This piece was in my family, I tell 'em. Been in my family for generations, it's damn well gonna stay there."

"I'd love to see it," Louise said.

Making herself sound interested. Why not?

"What's your name," Hank said.

She was going to suggest he goddamn well write it down.

"Louise," she said. "Louise Atkinson. What's your name?"

She picked up her rum and coke. Swizzled it with the red stick. Looked at the impaled red cherry.

"Hank Standish," he said. "It's a pleasure."

Vic was back to playing the Grass Roots.

Sooner or later love is gonna win.

"Does your wife ever wear the tiara? I mean like if you're going to do something very, very, special."

Hank laughed.

"More special than coming here, right?" Hank sounding smooth now. Not sober, but getting his act together.

Louise nodded.

"I guess," she said. "I mean this place is nice, I guess, but I meant like if you're going to a wedding or something. A formal event."

"She can't exactly wear it," Hank said. "Thing's encased in the Wedgwood. I thought I *explained* that. You can't tell what it is if you look at it."

Jimmy Frank flashed a look at Louise. Mock incredulity.

Louise suppressed a laugh.

"It's about yea big," Hank said.

He held up his hands twelve inches apart then narrowed them.

Jimmy Frank smiled. Held his own hands apart.

Louise saw him. Raised her eyebrows and shook her head.

"It's blue Wedgwood," Hank said. "On the bottom it's got a gold crown glazed on it with the note. Craziest thing you ever saw. Tell you the truth it's a little on the showy-showy side. Kinda looks like a carnival piece, if you follow me."

Hank looked at Louise's eyes. Seeing if she was following him.

She was.

"You might think it's an ashtray if you don't

know any better. Mother kept bobby pins in it."

Hank stopped.

He gazed into his glass of bourbon. Reflecting.

"I suppose we ought to keep the thing in the safe," he said, "but what the hell? Thing doesn't look like anything valuable. Probably explains why it never got pilfered in the first place."

❋ ❋ ❋

Hank signaled with two fingers. Came *this* close to snapping them.

Jimmy Frank brought the bottle, holding it by the neck.

He glanced at Louise.

"One for my friend, here," Hank said. He pointed at Louise. "One more for the lady."

Jimmy Frank shook his head.

Pilfered. Man talking about this tiara getting pilfered.

Jimmy Frank was used to hearing bullshit in this place, but this was something else.

How the man's family ended up with this tiara in the first place if pilfering hadn't been involved?

Louise put her hand over her glass. Looked over her shoulder.

"I'm fine," Louise said.

Jimmy Frank watched her. Louise picked up her purse. She was done with Hank. She looked around the bar.

"Smithsonian's not gonna lay their mitts on it,"

Hank said. "Uhn-uh. Doesn't matter what they offer me, I'm keeping it."

Hank was still talking. He hadn't given up.

"I've seen you play tennis, haven't I?" Hank said. "Out at the club, right? Aren't you the pro out there? You play a strong game. It's your attitude."

"I do," Louise said.

Tennis pro? Louise worked at a flower shop.

She said the words anyway. Nice and steady. Acknowledging a fact.

"I knew it," Hank said. "You're the women's pro. Am I right?"

"I'm a pro," Louise said. "Not that kind."

She looked at Hank again.

"Not that kind, either," she said.

Jimmy Frank turned away. Laughing.

"Stay right here," Hank said. He stood up. Adjusted his slacks. Headed toward the men's room.

Jimmy Frank was at the other end of the bar. Louise waved toward him. Something between a finger wave and Miss America. It looked good on her, anyway and she knew it.

"Time to settle up," she said.

"Uhn-uh," Jimmy Frank said. "No need for that."

He nodded toward the men's room.

"This is courtesy of our friend. Since you're a *pro*."

Louise laughed.

❊ ❊ ❊

When Hank Standish got back from the men's room, Louise was gone.

Hank focused on Jimmy Frank.

Held up one finger.

"Your name is Jimmy Frank," Hank said. Enunciating. "Jimmy Frank *Waters*."

Jimmy Frank nodded.

"That's right," he said.

"You play any ball in high school?" Hank said.

"Four years football and basketball," Jimmy Frank said.

"College?"

"Went on to the army,"

Hank nodded.

"One more the same way, Jimmy Frank," he said.

Jimmy Frank reached for the bourbon.

Hank Standish watched Jimmy Frank pour the drink. Knitted his brow.

"When's Herman coming back?" Hank said.

WE NEED
A LITTLE
CHRISTMAS

There is only one Johnny's Lunch in Cleveland and to find it you need to go around the corner from Coventry between Lancashire and Euclid Heights Boulevard in Cleveland Heights. This time of night, snow had covered parked cars up and down a dark street.

Neon letters defined a sign in Johnny's front window:

OPEN 24 HOURS A DAY.

Green light bathed the snow on the sidewalk in front. The diner looked like Edward Hopper's *Night Hawks* but not as busy.

Vic was the only customer at Johnny's. He sat in the far reaches with his back to the front door. A busboy mopped the front of the place. He put chairs on top of two tables and unfolded a *slippery-when-wet* sign. Vic had changed out of his piano bar tux. He wore a fringed buckskin jacket. His blonde hair fell over his eyes.

Vic looked like Dennis Hopper, no relation to Edward, in *Easy Rider*.

He was reading a paperback when Louise Atkinson came into Johnny's.

The hands on the diner's clock overlapped at ten minutes after two o'clock.

Vic slid deep into the booth giving Louise room.

Vic put down the novel. Louise glanced at the book. A white cover with red lettering and a samurai sword.

Shibumi, by Trevanian.

"What kind of book is that?" Louise said. "*Shibumi*? I don't get it."

Louise didn't wait for Vic's answer. She picked up the menu.

The samurai sword maybe made Vic's book look a *little* interesting.

"They need to change their menu," she said.

"Shibumi is a sort of state of perfection," Vic said. "It's a zen thing."

Louise tossed her menu away.

Management hadn't changed Johnny's Lunch over to Christmas yet. Circus animals still tromped around on the laminated menu as if they were auditioning for spots on a carousel.

The menu would have been perfect for a children's birthday party.

Louise pulled out a package of Virginia Slim cigarettes, took a sip of the graveyard-shift coffee.

Vic was making a pyramid with the plastic creamer collection. Keeping one eye on the snow coming down outside the glass front door.

A chummy rendition of *We Need a Little Christmas* piped from hidden speakers.

This was a new one, though. Louise had only heard it a few times. *Christmas Eve with Johnny Mathis.*

Candles in the window, carols on the spinet...

"You ever play this one?" Louise said.

"Play what?" Vic said.

Louise pointed over her head to a speaker nested in the ceiling.

"Do you play this song? *We Need a Little Christmas.* I never heard you play this one. It's catchy."

She sang a line.

Haul out the holly.

Making her voice tremble like Johnny Mathis.

"Unh-uh," Vic said. "I'll leave that one to you."

She told him about the tiara. Hank Standish in the bar.

Marie Antoinette.

"That's bar talk," Vic said.

They were quiet.

"Why are we here?" Louise said. "You aren't talking to me."

Vic shrugged.

He pushed the paperback an inch on the Formica table toward the creamers.

"Vic," Louise said. "You might as well tell me the truth."

"The truth?" Vic said. "What are you talking

about?"

"I'm talking about you and me kind of truth," Louise said. "Where we stand."

Vic still was working on the stack of creamers. Four of them stood one on top of the other like a totem pole. He pushed the second one, toppling them.

He shook his head.

"There's nothing to talk about, Louise," he said. "We don't stand anywhere. I'm done. This is the end of whatever you and me there ever was.

She looked at him. With unsteady hands took a cigarette from the pack.

"Well, she said, "at least I know."

"Jimmy Frank's coming," Vic said. "I asked him. He should be here any time."

"Wonderful," Louise said. "It's Christmas, right? The more the merrier."

It was over, Louise thought.

It was over and she wondered if it ever had really begun.

* * *

Jimmy Frank Waters came in the front door.

He walked to the booth, sat down across from Vic and next to Louise.

There was a book in front of Vic. They both had coffee.

The two of them were silent.

Jimmy Frank had taken time to change. Run into

his crib on his way up to Johnny's Lunch. Taken ten minutes to freshen up. Shower. Splash on some Ice Blue Aqua Velva.

He had taken off the bartender uniform from Eddie Swanson's Forest City Bar and Grill which was just a little too close to *Old Folks at Home* for Jimmy Frank's taste.

Put on his black ribbed turtleneck and his red leather jacket.

Together, the jacket, turtleneck, and Afro gave Jimmy Frank a nice solid look.

Louise had on a blue pantsuit. Not the same as she wore to Eddie Swanson's. She was looking good like she always did with wide lapels and a flowered blouse. Like *Charlie's Angels*.

Vic Collister was a lucky man.

All three had changed clothes after Eddie Swanson's, getting out of their working threads before coming to Johnny's.

The three of them sitting there, it wasn't *Charlie's Angels.* They looked more like *Mod Squad*.

"I'm definitely looking it up," Louise said.

Louise was animated. Acting like nothing had happened before Jimmy Frank came in.

"Whoa," Vic said. Held up his hand palm first toward Louise. "What're we talking about, now?"

"Come on," she said. "Get with it Vic, I just told you about the Marie Antoinette thing. What else would we be talking about?"

"I don't know," Vic said. "We could talk about the weather. You done all your Christmas shopping yet?

"Man. You're crazy," Jimmy Frank said. "Talking about all that."

"Biscuits and gravy are good," Vic said.

"You know I don't eat pork, Vic," Jimmy Frank. "Nine times out of ten you order biscuits and gravy you get pork."

"The tiara," Louise said.

Jimmy Frank looked at her.

"You talking about the thing at the bar?" Jimmy Frank said. Like there was some other tiara.

Louise looked him in the eyes. Shook her head.

Giving her hair the Cheryl Tiegs Clairesse shake.

Reached for the pack of Virginia Slims.

You've Come a Long Way Baby.

Took a cigarette.

Jimmy Frank laughed.

"I was just about to offer you one of mine," he said.

He took out a book of Eddie Swanson's Forest City matches and lit both their cigarettes.

Looked at Louise.

Vic picked up the book. Opened it.

Shibumi.

Jimmy Frank looked at Vic and the book.

"The hell kind of book is this, Vic?"

Jimmy Frank knew a man named Gates Miller who kept two samurai swords in his closet. Funny thing was, Gates Miller looked a lot like Gates Brown, the tubby outfielder used to play for the Detroit Tigers. Gates Miller brought the samurai swords back from his time serving in Okinawa. Gates Miller didn't want to tell Jimmy Frank how he'd gotten hold of them. After five minutes, though, Gates went ahead and told Jimmy Frank anyway.

The waitress put a glass of ice water in front of Louise.

"I'll come back in a minute," the waitress said.

"Take your time," Louise said.

Vic put down the book. Closed it.

"Fuck it," he said.

Called to the waitress. "Two chili dogs."

"There's pork in those, too," Jimmy Frank said.

"Like I give a shit," Vic said.

Jimmy Frank and Louise didn't say anything for a moment. They studied each other.

Jimmy Frank looked at Vic. Then looked at Louise again.

Louise was up to something.

Vic put the book down.

Then Jimmy Frank shook *his* head. Picked up his menu.

Louise looked at Vic.

Vic wasn't looking at her. He was trying to get the waitress's attention again.

Louise patted Jimmy Frank's hand.

They were the *Mod Squad* again.

Jimmy Frank put down his menu.

It was two thirty in the morning.

He looked at Louise, then back at Vic.

Jimmy Frank shook his head.

"Two of you are some kinda *trip*."

❊ ❊ ❊

Louise drove home. The snow was heavy.
Richard Harris was on the radio.
Someone left the cake out in the rain.
Louise shook her head. Lighted a cigarette.
She was driving too slowly.
The thing was, she should have known Vic didn't care about her.
She felt like an idiot. She needed something.

DAYS OF OUR LIVES

Louise was curious. That was all.

When she had gotten home last night, she'd gone to bed. But today was a new day.

She was thinking about the Wedgwood tiara.

To hell with Vic. She should have known better. She should have seen the handwriting on the wall. But it was too late to cry about Vic.

She was going to see what Hank Standish was talking about.

She wanted to see the tiara.

She wondered how long Vic had felt the way he did. Looking back, she could see he had never felt the same way about her as she felt about him. What the hell was wrong with her? Why hadn't she seen it? He was indifferent. She deserved somebody better than Vic.

She was thinking about the whole miserable mess with Vic, and she was thinking about Hank Standish's tiara.

Well, Marie Antoinette's tiara, if you were going to believe the story. If the tiara really had belonged to Marie Antoinette, why wasn't it in a museum?.

Louise couldn't get it out of her mind.

She had read about kleptomania in magazines and she was thankful she didn't have the condition. Louise wasn't any Woolworth's shoplifter.

Louise wasn't *any* kind of thief. Louise didn't want to *steal* the tiara. She had no intention of stealing anything at all.

She just wanted to see the tiara.

❈ ❈ ❈

Louise found Hank and Hilda Standish's address on Van Aken Boulevard.

Finding an address for the couple was easy. Hank and Hilda were listed in the Cleveland Social Register, and *that* volume was located in the cavernous *Special Collections* room at the Cleveland Public Library.

From the thousands of volumes in the public library, Louise needed only one tiny address. Louise loved the library. She loved the lions out in front, now dusted with snow. She loved the smell of the leather covered volumes. She loved finding Henry and Hilda Standish's address, right there on Van Aken Boulevard.

Louise took the Rapid to the library, found the address then went back to the florist shop.

She asked Larry for the employee discount on an arrangement of roses.

Forget sneaking anything out from under Larry's nose.

Larry *watched* his merchandise.

"We don't *have* an employee discount, honey," Larry said.

Louise did her best to look crestfallen.

Larry looked at her.

Louise quivered her lip.

"Fine," Larry said, "I'll take thirty percent off. Only because those roses are on their last legs."

Louise gave Larry the Mary Tyler Moore smile.

"What's the occasion?" he said.

"Oh, I forgot," Louise said, "it's a wedding. A big *family* wedding."

"This close to Christmas?" Larry said. "My *God,* what goes through people's minds?"

❋ ❋ ❋

The Standish's house on Van Aken was Tudor. Leaded windows and a pair of his and her turrets. A Christmas wreath festooned with glittering bells hung on the big front door. Louise stood beneath the stone porte-cochère. She held the bouquet of flowers in her yellow kidskin gloves. By now the flowers were close to frozen, but that was beside the point. She pushed the doorbell with her elbow.

Louise's short brunette wig made her look like Cousin Serena from *Bewitched*. It didn't matter who Louise looked like, as long as she didn't look like Louise Atkinson.

A woman wearing Keds sneakers and a tan running suit answered the door.

"I can't stop," Louise said. "I absolutely have to dash. If Hilda just has the teensiest minute…"

"Mrs. Standish isn't here," the woman said. Cigarette in one hand, a TV remote in the other.

The woman peeked around the flowers.

"She won't be back for a while. Maybe some time before Christmas."

Louise gasped.

"Oh my God," she said. "Nobody told me. I thought I was bringing the flowers *today*. The reception isn't today?"

"I don't know anything about any reception, honey," the woman said.

"May I come in for just the teensiest bit?" Louise said. "Oh my God, I think I'm going to faint."

The woman muttered something, but moved out of Louise's way.

"Suit yourself," she said. "You want me to get those flowers in some kinda vase? Your baby's breath is about to croak. I'm supposed to be keeping house, I might as well be doing something."

She took the flowers.

Louise shook her head.

"Oh, I guess not," she said. "I'll just backtrack. Find out where they actually belong."

"Looks like some nice flowers," the housekeeper said. "Be a shame to see them go to waste."

"You're so kind," Louise said. "I can't smell them, right now. I've lost my sense of smell."

"Same thing happened to my husband's mother," the housekeeper said. "It's a small world. Charlie's mother lost her smeller and then she went downhill from there. You got any other symptoms?"

Louise shook her head.

"I'm just kinda cold, I guess," Louise said.

"Maybe I could get you a little coffee?" the housekeeper said. "I was gonna do the rugs, but my dogs are killing me even in my sneakers. I'm gonna say the hell with the rugs."

"Oh, you poor thing," Louise said. "Maybe I should be getting coffee for you."

The housekeeper shook her head.

"Mrs. Standish wouldn't like that," she said. "Tell you the truth, the hell with coffee. How about some sherry?"

Louise smiled.

"That would be absolutely wonderful," she said. "Just the tiniest smidge would be nice."

An hour later, both women sat in leather chairs in the library opposite the walnut Curtis Mathes television console watching a game show hosted by Joe Garagiola.

The wedding flowers were arranged in a silver champagne bucket next to a bottle of sherry.

"Harvey's Bristol Cream," the housekeeper said, "the best there is."

Louise insisted on doing the pouring. It was the

least she could do.

The housekeeper liked sherry. After four glasses, the housekeeper flipped up the stereo lid the console and grabbed an album.

"Remember this one?" she said. "*Me Japanese Boy, I Love You*. Bobby Goldsboro. Don't you love it?"

Louise clapped her hands together.

"Oh I do," she said. "I absolutely am in love with Bobby Goldsboro. Everything he's ever done, I think."

"Me too," the housekeeper said. "I'm crazy about oriental music. You like *Sukiyaki*?"

"*Sukiyaki* too," Louise said. "*Sukiyaki* is absolutely dreamy."

After another sherry, the housekeeper started to talk about Hilda and Hank .

"He should just move on down there with her," the housekeeper said. "Even though that would put me out of a job, such as it is. The two kids haven't darkened these doors since beginning of summer and that was just in passing."

"Kids," Louise said. "What're you gonna do?"

"You're just a kid yourself," the housekeeper said, "you should talk."

Louise laughed. Reached for the bottle. Filled the housekeeper's glass again.

She hadn't touched her own glass, but the sherry was nearly empty.

"You know," Louise said. "I remember the first time I ever had brandy."

"This isn't brandy," the housekeeper said. "This

is Harvey's Bristol Cream.

She stood up. Not steadily.

"You want brandy, I'll bring some out. Boy do we have *brandy*."

"I don't want to bother you," Louise said.

"It's no bother, sweetie," the housekeeper said. "Don't you want to take off your coat and your gloves?"

She pointed at the yellow gloves.

Louise shook her head. Held up her hands.

"I just can't, she said. "I've got the worst rash. You wouldn't believe it."

An hourglass appeared on the screen. *Days of Our Lives* was on.

The housekeeper got to her feet.

"Well," she said, "they are stylish. I'll say that much."

"I will take off my coat, though," Louise said. She kept her coat on.

"Don't move," the housekeeper said. Pointed at the floor. "Stay right there."

Louise flipped through the collection of the albums.

Pulled out a Jackie Gleason.

Champagne, Candlelight, and Kisses.

She turned the stereo off. Turned up the television volume. Glanced at the album cover Louise held.

"Boy, *that's* a moldy oldy," the housekeeper said.

She had turned full attention toward the television.

"This is my show," she said. "I just love it. I think I've watched it ever since John Kennedy was in office. Do you ever watch it?"

"I do," Louise said. "I've missed some episodes recently."

"I can catch you up," the housekeeper said.

"Won't Mr. Standish be getting home soon?" Louise said.

"Don't worry about Hank. He never comes home until late," the housekeeper said. "I never even see him. I'm gone by the time he comes home. He goes directly from his office to the bar. Tell you the truth, I don't see why he even keeps an office. It's just a place for him to go before his four martooni lunch."

"Four martoonis?" Louise said. Laughed. "That's hilarious."

The housekeeper nodded. Laughed. Reached for the nearly empty bottle of sherry again. Tipped it toward Louise who shook the offer off.

"I forgot, I'm getting the brandy," the housekeeper said. "You like Dean Martin?"

Louise nodded.

"I absolutely adore Dean Martin," Louise said.

"Dean Martin says martooni instead of martini," the housekeeper said. Giggling. "Him or Foster Brooks. Oh hell, like you even care."

"That's hysterical," Louise said. "You are an absolute scream."

She put the album cover down. Looked at the housekeeper.

"So, Hank goes out every night?"

The housekeeper looked at Louise. Cocked her eyebrow.

"Uh-huh," she said. "Eddie Swanson's. Hank's home away from home."

The woman's feet were up. She had kicked off her Keds. Her mouth had formed a small o. She would be asleep for a couple of hours.

Louise stood up. Walked up the L-shaped staircase to the upstairs bedrooms. In the master bedroom a chesterfield dresser held an RCA Colortrak tuned to *Days of Our Lives.* Marlena Evans talking to a man Louise didn't recognize. A serious conversation about money. Louise didn't have time to concern herself with the show.

The Wedgwood tiara was next to the television. The tiara looked like an ashtray, although more ornate.

Louise picked it up. Held the tiara in her gloved hands. Shook it. She heard a rattle. Maybe it had belonged to Marie Antoinette. Maybe it hadn't.

Louise put the tiara in her purse.

Walked down the stairs. Looked at the housekeeper who would be asleep for a while. Louise let herself out of the house.

Walked down the street. Back to the Rapid.

EASY AL'S FIVE DOLLAR PARKING

Easy Al's Five Dollar Parking was a few steps from Eddie Swanson's. After leaving the Standish house on Van Aken, Louise pulled the Volare into Easy Al's. She opened her purse, looking for her lipstick.

Normally, Louise would have parked on the street, but the plows were coming and she was in a hurry. She would just have to pay for the parking. At least the car would be accessible when she came out. She clutched her coat to her chest. There was nothing she could do about her legs. They were cold.

Louise gave the keys to the Volare to Jackie Dunne.

He took the keys.

"I'll park it," he said. "Plenty of room in here."

"The thing is," Louise said, "I don't know how long I'll be. I guess it depends."

"That's okay whatever happens," Jackie said. "Man, it's cold out, though. Are you going to be warm enough?"

"I'm okay," she said. "I'm just going down the street. How about you, though? You're out in this all night. What a mess."

Jackie pointed at the shack.

"We got a heater in there. It warms up good. I'm okay."

"Well," she said, "if you're not here when I'm back, Merry Christmas."

Jackie nodded.

"Same to you," he said.

BASIC CHEMISTRY

Hank Standish wasn't going to drink very much tonight. And when Hank planned, he could keep his drinking in check.

He was pacing himself. An old history professor once told Hank that if he drank just one ounce of bourbon every fifty minutes, he could maintain his composure for an entire evening. The professor said it was just basic chemistry. The professor sounded like he knew what he was doing, although he did look pretty hungover every once in a while.

It helped that the regular man, Herm Taylor was back behind the bar.

Herm knew how to tend a bar. Not that Hank had anything against the other guy. Jimmy Frank Waters, that was his name. Not that Hank minded Jimmy Frank. He just liked Herm better.

Hank checked his watch. Forty minutes had passed since the first shot.

He signaled to Herm.

Hilda had called Hank at the office from Florida.

"Forget it, Hank," Hilda said, "I'm not coming back for Christmas. It's just too nice here. I play tennis in the morning, lie on the beach in the afternoon. I have no reason in the world to hurry home.

"That's all right with me," Hank said.

Hank decided he would go into the dining room tonight. They carved decent roast beef here at Eddie Swanson's. A change from frozen Stouffer's.

He looked next to him.

Louise had appeared out of nowhere.

"Boy am I glad to see you," he said.

❋ ❋ ❋

Louise Atkinson ditched the Serena wig before going to Eddie Swanson's.

Hank Standish stood at the same place at the bar. Like he was expecting her.

Herm Taylor behind the bar.

Herm looked and sounded like Sammy Davis Jr.

Louise looked at Hank. Smiled. Hank really wasn't a bad looking guy and tonight he wasn't tight.

"It's good to see you," she said. "I'm kinda surprised you remember me."

"You're kidding me, right?" Hank said. "Louise."

Making a point to show he knew her name.

"I never forget a pretty face."

"You say that to all the girls, don't you?" she said.

"No, I don't," he said. "Just pretty ones I'm about

to ask to dinner."

"I'm waiting for somebody," she said.

Hank pointed at the dining room.

"The piano man, right?" he said.

Louise nodded. Took out a Virginia Slim.

Hank lighted it using a paper match from the bar.

"I'm not making a pass," he said. "Don't worry about that part."

She laughed.

"You're not?" she said. "I'm not so sure how I should take that."

"I'm absolutely not," Hank said. "I'm more or less happily married to a woman who currently is more or less happily living in Florida."

"I don't blame her," Louise said.

"Blame her for staying in Florida or for being happy?" Hank said.

Louise inhaled the cigarette.

"Just dinner?" she said.

"Why not? I know a place in Murray Hill makes a damn fine cacciatore. You up for that?" Hank said. Ditching the idea of Eddie Swanson's roast.

He looked at her.

"You drive if that makes you feel more comfortable. My car or yours?"

"I'll drive myself," she said. "I'll follow you."

SLAVIC LOLLOBRIGIDA

The Samovar was a belly dancing place. As good a place as any for a diamond scam.

Natasha was chatting with another of the dancers. Hal spotted her when the woman at the door pointed at her. Hal saw why she had gotten Eggy's attention.

"She's dancing in a minute," the woman said.

Natasha wore leopard print pants and a yellow cropped top.

She wasn't any Lollobrigida, either. She was lithe, like Mitch Walczak's favorite, Juliet Prowse.

Natasha's body was proportional. Hal had pictured her differently when he heard Eggy talking about her.

Fortunately the heat in the *Samovar* was on.

At least she wasn't *Boris and Natasha* Russian. This Natasha had been in this country long enough to sound like anyone else.

She looked at Hal's badge and sat down with him in a seat in the back of the *Samovar*.

"Somewhere we won't get interrupted," she said.

The booth was surrounded by Indian print fabrics.

Hal's knees were on a level with his chin when he spoke to her.

It turned out her name wasn't Natasha. This did not come completely as a surprise to Hal.

Her name was Susan Slonimsky.

Not that complicated a name, really.

Hal also wasn't surprised she hadn't used the name in her conversations with Eggy.

"My parents wanted me to have an American name," Susan said. "Like people couldn't tell I wasn't just a little Russian girl with the name Slonimsky.

"I was just having a little fun with Eggy. Then my boyfriend finds out he's coming here and he finds out about Eggy."

"Your boyfriend?" Hal said.

"Max," Susan said. "He's out front, in case the customers get ideas."

"He wouldn't be the guy Eggy thought was your uncle?"

Susan laughed.

"Eggy's something," she said. "He wouldn't believe me when I told him I wasn't really from Russia. He wanted to believe what he wanted to believe."

"Can you get Max to come in here?" Hal said. "I wanna talk to both of you."

"Suit yourself," Susan said. She left and came back with Max. Max was half Hal's size. He wore a black shirt and a red tie. His shoes were pointed.

This was the uncle?

"I got somebody for you to meet," Hal said.

"Oh yeah?" Susan said. "A friend of Eggy's?"

Hal shook his head. Looked at his watch.

"Look," he said. "He's outside right now, but I'm gonna get him."

"Whatever you say, pal," Max said. "We got nothing to hide."

Hal went outside. He walked to the corner. Lighted a cigarette and knocked on the hood of his car.

Gave a come-on-in motion.

Max and Susan were sitting next to each other in the booth when he returned.

Hal puffed on the cigarette.

"I thought you were bringing a mystery man with you?" Susan said.

Hal walked into the booth and stepped sideways.

Stan Mandarich stood behind Hal dressed in his Boris Kolenkhov costume from *You Can't Take it With You.*

Six foot eight in his stocking feet.

At least two sixty, Hal estimated.

Maybe more but he'd never gotten him on a scale.

Stan was a hell of an actor.

He was angry.

"Where's the Russian?" Stan said.

"Easy, Boris," Hal said. He pointed at Max. "This guy here. He says he's got nothing to hide."

Stan wore high black boots. Probably left over from the days in the ring as one of the Masked

Magicians.

With the same effort as picking out a tissue, Stan picked up Max and held him over his head. Started twirling him around like a propeller. Max's pointed shoes went round and round.

"I got no money," Max said. "Leave me alone. Put me down for crying out loud. My heart isn't strong."

"I slam him into the corner turnbuckle," Stan said. "Then, *body slam* is next for him."

Hal watched. Smoking his cigarette.

"Okay," Max said. "I might have some money. Not all of it. Just some."

Hal signaled. Stan lowered Max.

He was surprised Stan hadn't gone farther in wrestling.

He was a pro.

MARY TYLER MOORE

Jackie Dunne saw her coming back.

"Getting your car back?" he said. "That was fast."

Louise smiled. He looked like the guy on *Taxi*. Tony something. Hooded sweatshirt under a puffy down jacket. Louise wondered what the attendant's name was.

"Change of plans," she said.

"I'm not charging you," he said.

"Thanks," she said. "You're a sweetheart."

She watched him bring out the Volare.

He moved cars fast, like he wasn't looking.

"Here you go," he said. Handed her the keys.

"What's your name?" she said.

"Jackie," he said.

"Mine's Louise," she said.

"Nice meeting you, Louise," Jackie said. "Maybe I'll see you around."

"I work at the florist shop next to the Terminal Tower," she said.

"Nice," Jackie said.

"I mean," she said, "I kinda owe you one. If

you need some flowers, you know, I could use my employee discount."

"Thanks," Jackie said. "You never know."

"Be seeing you," Louise said.

❊ ❊ ❊

Conn Rutherford watched Jackie Dunne come back into the shack at Easy Al's Parking Lot.

The woman in the Volare had made a fuss over Jackie. You could tell she had her eye on Jackie by the way she'd watched him backing the car out.

She'd only been parked for about twenty minutes.

She'd gone down to Eddie Swanson's then right back. If she'd been there ten minutes Conn would have been surprised.

Short skirt, high boots, a nice fur jacket.

Still, she looked wholesome. She was like Mary Tyler Moore tossing her hat into the air.

Conn asked Jackie if she'd tipped. Jackie shrugged.

"Shoulda gotten her number, anyway, Jackie," Conn said. "She looks just like Mary Tyler Moore. And she was looking you over. You coulda got her number."

Jackie shrugged.

"Maybe I coulda," he said.

Jackie was still young.

You get those opportunities, you need to take them.

"Maybe she wasn't your type," Conn said. "Was

that it? She wasn't your type?"

"No, she was fine, Conn," Jackie said. "She'll be back."

Conn shook his head. The kid had a few things to learn yet. He reached for a Strohs in the paper bag under the counter.

MAMA LEONE'S

Hank Standish and Louise were at Mamma Leone's on Mayfield. Hank Standish ordering the cacciatore and a bottle of chianti. Louise ordered a salad.

"So," Louise said. "You want to show me your etchings, right?"

"Etchings? Yeah it's a little like that," Hank said. Smooth now. Acting different than the other night. Not smashed for one thing. At least he wasn't showing it.

*   *   *

When the waiter came offering dessert, Hank waved him off. He invited Louise to his house for a nightcap. He would show her the tiara, nothing else.

"You can follow me in your own car," he said. "I'll drive nice and easy. Just like Frank Sinatra, right? *Nice and easy does it.* I don't know. Does your boyfriend do that one? If I get pulled over, you just go on ahead. No need to be involved with anything like that."

"Sure, Louise said. "I'm game."

Part two of the plan *depended* on going to Hank's house. Get Hank to put a couple of logs on the fire. Loosen up a little. Get comfy with his shoes off and all.

She had a little grass in her purse. Maybe Hank wasn't as square as he looked.

"Pull up to the side of the place," Hank had said.

He parked his Benz in the circular drive. Nice car, maybe white, although hard to say in the dark and in the snow.

❋ ❋ ❋

The chintz couch was comfy. Just like before. No sign of the housekeeper. Hank put on some Cannonball Adderley. *Sukiyaki* and Bobby Goldsboro were not in sight. The housekeeper must have kept those albums elsewhere.

"You like jazz," he said.

"Oh I do," she said. "Got any Miles?"

"Good taste," he said.

❋ ❋ ❋

"Just wait here," Hank said. "I'll bring it down."

She looked at him.

"You're bringing the tiara down here?" she said. "I'm not supposed to go up there?"

"Uhn-uh," he said. "This is just gonna take a

minute."

He got up from the couch, slid a *Body by Fisher* coaster under his drink. He took off his loafers, exposing a pair of argyle socks.

Held up his finger toward Louise.

"I'll be right back."

Like she was going anywhere.

She might make a quick trip into the kitchen to dump her drink into the sink.

But she needed to see how Hank reacted to the tiara being gone.

"Make yourself at home," he said.

She watched him trudge up the L-shaped staircase. Heard him walk down the hardwood floor upstairs.

She got up, went to the kitchen and emptied most of her drink. Glanced for a second at a shelf filled with cookbooks.

Larousse Gastronomique. Paul Bocuse. Julia Child. The Galloping Gourmet.

Gourmet Magazines stacked on the shelf underneath. A vase with dead flowers just sitting there.

The ones she had brought.

"Damn thing's not up there," Hank said. "I'll have to talk to the housekeeper tomorrow."

"It's not there?" Louise said. "You think she put it someplace else?"

"Unh-uh," Hank said. "Negatory. The thing gets dusted sometimes, but it never gets moved."

"Weird," Louise said. "Well, I guess we can

always look at your etchings."

He sat back down on the couch. Picked up the drink and looked at the mostly melted ice.

"I got no etchings," he said.

"I knew that," she said.

He leaned back, held the drink toward Louise.

She picked up what was left of hers.

"Well, what the hell?" he said. "Cheers."

"Cheers, she said.

"You aren't really a tennis pro after all," he said.

"No," she said, "not even close."

"Hell," he said. "I remembered. It just came to me. You know how that happens? Where I've seen you."

She didn't say anything.

"You work at that florist place. Near Higbees."

Louise shook her head.

"Maybe it's somebody who looks like me."

Hank smiled. Nodded slightly.

They were both quiet then.

Watching the flames dance in the fire.

"Well," he said, "this was kind of a flop. I already told you I wasn't making a pass so I won't. Not even a little one."

Hank put his arm up and over her shoulder. She felt his hand on the top part of her arm. He really wasn't a bad guy.

His head nodded down toward his chin.

Louise took the drink from his hands and placed it on top of the *Body by Fisher* coaster. She stood up and walked toward the fireplace. The logs were blazing. She made sure the screen covered the fire entirely. She went to the banister where Hank had put her coat and picked it up.

Miles Davis was playing *So What* on the Pioneer turntable. Hank had put the album on repeat.

Bah dah bi dee bah... BAH buh.

Bah dah bi dee bah... BAH buh.

Louise didn't look back at the couch. Hank's eyes were open. Watching her. She left, closing the door carefully behind her.

SILVER BELLS

Hilda's phone call took Hank by surprise.

She was coming home.

"I'm coming back, Hank," she said. "I mean, what the hell am I doing, right? Christmas down here? It's seventy degrees, there's not a cloud in the sky. I can walk on the beach every day. I can play tennis outside. But..."

"But what?" Hank said.

"Damn it, Hank," she said. "I miss you."

"I'm glad," he said. He still had plenty of Stouffer's frozen dinners, but he would be glad to see Hilda. He missed her. Still, Hank had to do something about the tiara before Hilda got home.

Hank needed to do something about Louise, too.

He didn't know about Louise. He liked her, but he smelled a rat when the tiara was gone.

And, the whole situation would be hard to explain to Hilda. Hilda might have warm nostalgic feelings now, while in sunny Florida, but her mood could change.

Louise was hard to figure.

Hank knew three things for sure.

One, he didn't want to get taken for a ride.

Two, he didn't want Hilda to get wind of the

business with Louise.

Three, he needed to put his eyes on the tiara.

Hank Standish knew a guy downtown who took care of things. This situation had Gerry Joyce's name written all over it.

MARTINIS AND STRIPPERS

Hank knew Gerry Joyce could help him.

Hilda herself had used Gerry's services when Hank got involved with a stripper who worked in a place close to 9th on Short Vincent. Gerry was an effective, though unlicensed, private investigator. From the start, Hank knew getting involved with Tawny Landers was a bad idea but he hadn't been able to untangle himself.

Hank wasn't sure how Hilda found Gerry. Maybe one of her Junior League friends. It didn't matter how Hilda found Gerry. Gerry had talked sense into Hank and gotten the situation resolved.

Hank never harbored hard feelings toward Gerry. Far from it. Hank was grateful to Gerry. He didn't want to lose Hilda and he saw, once the martini-fueled affair was over, how Tawny Landers could have taken everything Hank was good for. Hank had sworn off martinis after the experience. Martinis spelled nothing but trouble. Martinis and strippers.

"You wanna be careful with strippers as a rule,

Hank," Gerry said.

He was a few years older than Hank and enjoyed giving fatherly advice.

"Look at Miss Landers as a well turned-out carny. She never had your best interests at heart."

* * *

Gerry Joyce wasn't surprised seeing Hank come into his shop. Wearing bluejeans and a gray *GARDA* sweatshirt, Gerry stopped pounding his speed bag when Hank came in. He listened to Hank's story about the missing tiara and Louise.

"So you were running your mouth again then, were you Hank?" Gerry said.

Hank, hungover and embarrassed, shook his head

"I didn't think she was listening too carefully," he said. "Listen, I'm not a hundred percent sure she took the thing."

"But you came to see old Gerry Joyce anyway, didn't you?" Gerry said. Enjoying this.

Watching Hank squirm was a bit of good craic.

"You're getting older, Hank," Gerry said. "We all are. But why are you still drinking? You can't handle the stuff. I think we've established that."

Hank hung his head.

"I've slowed down."

Gerry closed his eyes. He held the palm of his gnarled hand toward Hank. Shook his head.

"Be that as it may, Hank," he said. "The question

is what to do now, isn't it? That's why you're here."

Hank was miserable.

"Oh hell," Gerry said. "No need to be glum, lad. I'll look into this little matter and call you later."

Hank nodded. Fumbled for his wallet.

"Look," Gerry said. Almost apologetic. "Price will be a little higher now than when I helped Hilda."

Hank nodded.

"Inflation," he said. "We should have kept Gerald Ford in office. *Whip Inflation Now*. That was smart economic policy."

"It's that," Gerry said, "but I'll also be having a young man working with me."

"Somebody else?" Hank said. On his guard, but trying not to sound suspicious.

"A younger fella," Gerry said. "Fresh legs you might say. Nothing to worry about. Hal Bailey's his name. Very competent. Very trustworthy."

MACARTHUR'S PARK

Louise Atkinson saw the tall man as soon as he walked into the flower shop. She would have seen him immediately even if the little bell hadn't jangled.

Louise's boss, Larry Carmichael, told her to go ahead and help the guy.

Larry was busy working on a late-fall arrangement. Larry hated these orders. He was sputtering. Everything was set for Christmas now and somebody has to call up and want chrysanthemums again.

The customer had to be six foot six. He had a permanent sunburn and a hawk-like nose similar to Ken Harrelson's.

Handsome in a way. Louise liked the way his hair hung down over the back of his collar. Kind of a Prince Valiant look. Confident but not cocky.

Wearing canary slacks in winter, though.

Black fur coat and a pair of white leather Converse basketball shoes.

"Can I help you?" Louise said.

"You're Louise Atkinson," the man said.

Louise looked over at Larry Carmichael who was still fussing over the arrangement.

The guy sounded like a cop.

"If they tell me they want hostas in this thing, I'm gonna scream," Larry said. "Don't tell me they want hostas."

Silver Bells played on the MUZAK loop.

"That's me," Louise said, "I'm Louise."

"Uh, great," the man said. He pulled a leather case from his coat pocket. There was a badge inside the case. The badge was shaped like the state of Ohio.

"My name's Hal Bailey," the man said. He turned so Larry Carmichael couldn't look at them.

"If you're Louise Atkinson, I gotta have a chat with you."

❊ ❊ ❊

Hal and Louise sat across from each other at the Rumpus Room.

Louise made it clear, she didn't have the tiara, if there even was such a thing.

Hal asked her about Hank Standish. And the tiara.

"I heard him talking about it," Louise said. "So could anyone else who was listening."

"Lot of people in there?" Hal said. Playing it straight.

"You know the place?" she said. "You know Eddie Swanson's?"

"Eddie Swanson's Forest City," Hal said. "I guess that's the swankiest place left on Short Vincent."

"It's always busy," Louise said.

"You shoulda seen it in the old days. Short Vincent, right? The whole street used to really be busy back a few years ago." Hal was massaging his knee "White tablecloths they got in that place.

Louise watched him.

"It's an old basketball injury," he said. "Thing is, I don't have the range of motion I used to. Not nearly."

"Maybe it's early arthritis," Louise said. "You're tall. That happens. I took you for a basketball player right away."

"I played some," Hal said. "I don't believe in false modesty. Once upon a time, I got a few Mid-American college offers, on account of my first step. I had a crossover that could break your ankles if you're guarding me."

"I'll make a note," Louise said.

"Listen, Louise," Hal said. "We're pretty sure you know something about the tiara. This is your chance to come clean about it."

Louise shook her head.

"We talked to the housekeeper," Hal said. "She didn't feel all that great in the first place, on account of I think she was pretty hungover. But she also wasn't feeling great about Hank Standish asking her what happened to the item in question."

"His housekeeper?"

"She gave me a description," Hal said. "It was pretty accurate. I mean, she even mentioned the yellow gloves. She was pretty unhappy."

"Shit," Louise said.

"So, what really happened?" Hal said.

Louise went through the story about meeting Hank Standish at Eddie Swanson's. Her boyfriend played piano there. Vic Collister. They weren't exactly boyfriend-girlfriend, but close. Well, now they weren't exactly anything, but that was a different story.

She went to Hank's house the next night.

That was when Hank told her the tiara was missing.

"You think he knew about it being gone before you came over?" Hal said.

Louise shook her head.

"That wouldn't make sense.

"That fits with what Hank said to us," Hal said.

"He reported me?" Louise said. "To who?"

"That's not exactly what happened," Hal said. "He didn't exactly *quote unquote* report you. Listen, Louise. You want something good? Try the Old Fashioned they got here."

"Thanks," Louise said. "I'm fine with beer. You're not police?"

Hal looked at her.

"Not technically," he said. "My badge is for being a Licensed Bond Agent. I got a lot of friends in on the force though. I support them a hundred percent."

Louise nodded.

"Me too," she said. "They keep us safe."

Hal nodded. Reached for a cigarette.

"Licensed Bond Agent?" she said. "That's a new one on me."

"It's what I do," Hal said. "Closest thing I can say is I'm like a bounty hunter, but I don't like saying that on account of people start thinking I should be wearing buckskins or like that."

Louise pointed at the cigarette package.

"I'll take one," she said.

He passed her his pack and lit their cigarettes.

"So, did you end up playing basketball in college?"

Hal held his hand out, palm down. Wiggled it side to side.

"*Comme ci comme ça*, you might say," he said. "Kinda. I'll tell you what I did do, though. I got a pile of stuffed animals shooting free throws at county fairs summertime between junior and senior year. That was after the injury. I didn't know if I'd play senior year."

Louise sipped the foam from the top of the beer.

Looked at Hal.

He was laughing.

"You know, three shots for a dollar except the hoop's wrong. I got eighty-sixed from the midway most of the time I went. They got the hoops rigged. Didn't matter, I pissed the carnies off I won so many stuffed animals. They wrote an article about me in the Plain Dealer. *Free-Throw Whiz* they called me. I still got a newspaper picture of me at the Coshocton County Fair. I'm holding a basketball and a couple teddy bears."

"What did you do with the teddy bears," Louise said.

Hal shrugged.

"I didn't need them. I took them to the hospital. They gave them to kids, I guess."

"That was nice," she said. "You must be a nice guy. Listen, what's a nice guy like you talking about this stuff with me? This is something about Hank Standish? I don't know what I can tell you. He's also a nice guy. I think he's in love with his wife, which is sweet. I'm sorry about the tiara. I don't know what to do about it, though."

Hal nodded.

"It's nice to see a happy couple," he said, "especially in this day and age. I got a friend been married a hundred years. Then boom, out of the blue he's telling me him and his wife got a trial separation."

Hal shook his head.

"I didn't see that coming, even though the guy's kinda a schlub. Me, I think marriage should be for good."

"Like the songs?" she said.

"Yeah, like that," Hal said. "Anyway, Hank's in trouble and you can help."

"I could try," she said.

She looked at him.

"I can't imagine what I could do."

Hal smiled. He liked her look. Somewhere between surprise and remorse.

"Look," Hal said. "Hank isn't looking for a pound of flesh. He wants the tiara back before his wife gets back from Florida."

"I don't think I can help you," Louise said.

"You might be interested to know the thing is worth between about twenty-five dollars and maybe a hundred," Hal said. "Prolly closer to the lower figure."

Louise nodded. Tapped her cigarette in the ashtray.

"It didn't belong to Marie Antoinette?" she said.

Hal shook his head.

"Not even close."

Louise had a look on her face. Like she wasn't there.

"You know that song?" she said, "Richard Harris sang it. The actor."

"*MacArthur's Park*," Hal said.

"It's like that," Louise said. "You ever wonder what the words mean? I mean he's left a cake out in the rain."

"I think it's about the end of a relationship," Hal said.

"Exactly," she said. "I've been wandering around the last few days. I didn't know what I was doing. They play *MacArthur's Park* on the radio? It takes forever. It's full of drama, but in the end, what does it mean?"

"You had a relationship just end?" Hal said.

She nodded.

"I had a teacher in high school had us read parts of *Macbeth*," she said. "He went on and on about how life was just a tale told by an idiot. Full of sound and fury. Something like that. He went on and on about it. He liked the way the word idiot sounded, I guess."

"*Macbeth*," Hal said. "Shakespeare, right? I guess I wasn't in those kinda classes. I took jock lit."

"It wasn't even really a relationship," Louise said. "I just imagined it was, now I look at it."

"He's willing to pay you to help," Hal said.

Louise took another sip of her beer.

"He doesn't need to pay me," she said.

Hal looked at her.

"I was the idiot," she said. "And for nothing."

"Oh hell," Hal said, "don't beat yourself up over it. People do things all the time they wish they hadn't later.

"Thanks," she said, "I guess."

It's Christmas," he said.

She looked at him.

"You can get the tiara back to Hank?"

Hal nodded.

"Not me exactly," he said. "But leave it with me. I got a guy does deliveries."

WHISTLE FOR YOUR BEER

Herm Taylor had not exaggerated Fontana's abilities. Fontana was a very good safe cracker. A master of all trades, Fontana would have said, if asked, but particularly good at getting into a safe.

Bratenahl Deluxe Motors was a postage stamp sized car lot surrounded by orange and black plastic sale flags and covered by snow.

Looking out the window, Phil Fontana saw Jimmy Frank Waters.

Fontana, with the tweed fedora propped on the back on his head and the pipe clenched between his teeth was an exasperated Phil Silvers. Fontana single-handedly ran the two man car sales lot. The car lot was one of Fontana's several enterprises. The only legal one.

Once upon a time, another salesman sat at the desk opposite Fontana. Jerry Walters sold a fair number of cars and hadn't asked too many questions. Fontana had been surprised when Walters left his desk at ten o'clock on a Tuesday in September. Walters gave no previous clues to his departure. He just got up that day and told Fontana he was heading to Tucson. He wasn't going to put up with another winter in Cleveland.

Walters left everything on his desk including a brown 'whistle-for-your-beer' mug he brought from his home after a messy divorce. Fontana kept everything on his desk just the way Walters left it including a nearly finished cup of coffee and the flattened cellophane wrapper leftover from a Little Debbie Honey Bun.

Walters wasn't coming back, but Fontana didn't like an empty office.

* * *

Most of Fontana's cars were mousy Pintos, Vegas, and Chevettes in shades of brown, mustard, and mud. Since selling the Roadrunner to Collister, Fontana had two premium cars left. A Lincoln and a Challenger.

Jimmy Frank Waters had spotted the gold sparkle Lincoln Continental.

Fontana watched Jimmy Frank circle the Lincoln. He had never seen the man before.

Jimmy Frank glided around the lot, kicking the white-walls of the Lincoln one at a time.

The sparkle gold Continental was beautiful. Custom. A prime example of the Lincoln brand. Gold but not *too* gold. More like champagne.

Fontana came out of his office puffing his briar pipe. Hat properly cocked on his head. Feather smooshed nicely in the grosgrain band.

Fontana and Jimmy Frank exchanged pleasantries about the weather and the car.

The Lincoln was one-owner, Fontana said. The perfect car for the right person.

Phil Fontana studied Jimmy Frank.

Jimmy Frank maintaining his poker face. Body language showing interest.

"Car like this sells itself, doesn't it?" Fontana said. Slapped the hood with his pigskin glove.

"Mmm," Jimmy Frank said. Noncommittal.

Fontana took Jimmy Frank into the office in the office. Casual stuff. Just kicking numbers around.

Fontana bought the Lincoln the week before in Euclid Heights from the widow of a union bigwig. All the maintenance records were still in the glove container. The bigwig had been fastidious.

Fontana was prepared to show the yellow sheets of paper to a buyer.

The widow thought the Lincoln was showy. She felt ostentatious driving the car anywhere, even before her husband died. She didn't even want to drive the car to Fontana's car lot.

Fontana had made a house call.

"What does a gold Lincoln say about me?" she said.

Fontana figured the widow was entitled to her opinion. It was her car.

"Even I drive it to Fisher-Fazios, I feel like people stare."

When her husband died, the widow called

Bratenahl Deluxe Motors because of the prominent hand-painted sign:

Crazy Phil Buys Your Car
The Easy Way
For best CA$H price
$top in TODAY

Fontana was proud of the sign. Advertising paid.

Jimmy Frank nodded, looked at the car.

Staying nonchalant, digging the wheels.

"I wish I had ten of these cars," Fontana said. "I could sell every last one of them. This is a Florida car, that's what this is."

Jimmy Frank touched the hood of the car. Already feeling ownership.

"Come on in here where it's warm, Jimmy Frank, this is a very typical Cleveland winter," Fontana said.

He held the door to his office open. Jimmy Frank walked in first. Looked around at pictures of golf holes on the wall.

Jimmy Frank looked at Fontana holding the door open for him. *Sergeant Bilko*.

"I got the heat up high and the prices down low," Fontana said.

"Uh-huh," Jimmy Frank said.

Under his breath but still audible.

Fontana closed the door behind Jimmy Frank.

Jimmy Frank stamped snow from his shoes.

"You Crazy Phil?"

Fontana stuck out his tongue. Waved his hands around his head.

Grinned.

"Guilty as charged," he said.

Fontana brought out a typed sheet listing the attributes of the 1974 Lincoln.

All business now.

Clean title. Oversized hide-away headlights, custom rims, light-up curb feelers. Fontana was prepared to talk air conditioning, mufflers, whatever he needed to talk about.

"You like, I can throw in a sound system. Custom however way you like it," Fontana said.

Jimmy Frank nodded.

"Mmm-hmm."

"Some people like more bass," Fontana said.

Hinting.

"However you like, it's up to you."

"Bass gotta thump," Jimmy Frank said. "Like Bootsy."

Fontana grinned.

"Glad you brought up Bootsy, Jimmy Frank," Fontana said. "Shows you got taste."

There were two desks in the room. Fontana had Jimmy Frank sit at the clean one.

No clutter for Phil Fontana.

No pictures, no knickknacks, no nothing.

Jimmy Frank wanted the car.

"You like the car," Fontana said, "I can tell you like it. It fits you real good, too. Tall man like you needs leg room. The other thing, Jimmy Frank? You don't have to worry about anybody else having a car like this. There ain't another one like this.

Even the gold sparkle is custom. You ready to drive it away?"

Fontana hadn't even sat down. His hat was dusted with snow and so was the feather.

Jimmy Frank squinted. His legs were spread out wide.

"You got a sign out there says payday payments, right?" Jimmy Frank said.

Fontana cocked his head. Gave Jimmy Frank a quizzical look.

As if this was news.

Jimmy Frank pointed at the snowy parking lot. Colored sales flags were strung along the street. The marquee lettered sign offered payday payments.

No Credit
Low Credit
No Problem
Payday Payments

"That one," Jimmy Frank said. "Sign says payday payment."

Fontana grinned. Looked at Jimmy Frank. Pulled out an application.

"Absolutely," he said. "That's what the sign says. Let's run through this. What do you do for work, Jimmy Frank?"

Jimmy Frank looked at Fontana. Smiled.

"I prefer not to say."

Practiced.

Just like he was asking to call his lawyer. Jimmy Frank stretched back in the chair so Fontana could see the gun under Jimmy Frank's jacket.

A Smith and Wesson .44.

The most powerful handgun in the world, right?

Fontana looked at the gun. Looked at Jimmy Frank.

He wadded the credit application into a ball and threw a clean-as-a-whistle seven foot rainbow shot into the garbage basket by the other desk.

"Just like Austin Carr. 61 points in the NCAA tournament, right?" Fontana said. "No dunks. No three-pointers."

Jimmy Frank watched Fontana. Nodded.

"I got a proposal," Jimmy Frank said. "I might wanna take the car, but I got something more interesting to discuss. I got your name from a mutual acquaintance. You know a man named Herm Taylor?"

Fontana stood up. He turned around, walked to the door of the office and opened it. Looked outside in both directions. Satisfied nobody else was close to the building, he shut the door.

Locked it.

Slipped in the bolt.

Flipped the cardboard hanger in the door window. Snapped his fingers.

We are Open had turned to *We are Closed* in a blink.

Fontana came back and sat opposite Jimmy Frank.

"Jimmy Frank," Fontana said, "I am obliged to ask if you are connected in any way with law enforcement? By that I am including all levels of city, state, and federal."

Jimmy Frank smiled.

"Uhn-uh," he said. "Do I look like the man?"

"No you do not. But I have to ask you," Fontana said. "I just gotta cover my ass with some due diligence."

Jimmy Frank nodded.

"How 'bout you," Jimmy Frank said. "You the fuzz?"

Fontana put the fingertips of both hands to his chest then pushed the hat back on his head.

"Me?" he said.

He smiled. Phil Silvers again.

"I'm as far from fuzz as you can get. Just ask Herm."

Fontana leaned back in his chair.

Tweed fedora still on, still making eye-contact.

Jimmy Frank doing the talking.

"Herm says you got some skills. Says you can bust a safe open. Says you got contacts buying and selling." Fontana shrugged.

"In addition to all that, my friend, I got modesty."

Fontana studied Jimmy Frank's face. Jimmy Frank giving away nothing.

"Seriously, it all depends," Fontana said. "Times change. Values change. Who knows? What do you have?"

"A damn treasure is what I got," Jimmy Frank said. "Locked up in a safe. That's where you come in."

Fontana nodded.

"It's good to know your limitations.."

"Herm says you're the best."

"Again, it depends," Fontana said. "What are we talking? Gold, bonds, what?"

Jimmy Frank squared his legs in front of himself, bridged his fingers. Looked into Fontana's eyes.

"I tell you this, and this gets back to me, you don't wanna see no part of me coming."

"Right," Fontana said. "I understand this part. That's a standard concern. Don't worry, though. What we got is like lawyer-client. Priest-penitent. Pretty much sacred."

Jimmy Frank nodded.

"Just wanted to clear that up ahead of time."

"Sensible," Fontana said. "Working arrangements should always be based on mutual trust. I insist on it."

Fontana paused.

Touched the tweed fedora. Took the hat off and inspected the little feather and the grosgrain band.

"Sometimes," Fontana said, "sometimes if you got somebody on the inside, you can work the *unfaithful watchman* game. Ever heard of that?"

Jimmy Frank shook his head no.

Fontana smiled.

"That just means the guy who's working there lets you in. That play's as old as the hills, but it can work like a charm if your guy has any kind of acting ability. Otherwise, he's looking at getting his goose cooked early."

Jimmy Frank looked at him. Pulled a cigarette and a black and gold matchbook from his shirt pocket. Lighted the cigarette and took a deep puff. Exhaled in the direction of Fontana.

Clunked his *Taking Care of Business* ring on the side of Fontana's desk.

"I got nobody on the inside," Jimmy Frank said. "I meant this to be a one man job, but I can't do a safe."

"You an Elvis man?" Fontana said. He nodded toward Jimmy Frank's ring.

"James Brown himself talks about Elvis," Jimmy Frank said. "Man could put on a show."

Fontana stood up. Took an ashtray from the other desk and put it in front of Jimmy Frank. Took his briar pipe from his coat pocket.

"I smoke these," he said. "Ever try a pipe? They broke me of the cigarette habit, although sometimes I'm tempted."

Jimmy Frank nodded.

Like he was going to smoke a pipe.

"I got a safe I need opened," Jimmy Frank said. "Split the take fifty-fifty."

"I'm intrigued," Fontana said.

Made a rolling tell-me-more motion with his hand.

Jimmy Frank smiled. He liked this.

FUNERAL HOME

Jimmy Frank Waters and Herm Taylor were freezing. Standing on one foot then standing on the other in front of the Johnson Brother's business.

Fontana was fifteen minutes late.

"Damn, brother," Herm Taylor said, "We doing this thing sometime this year, or what?"

The night was cold. Light snow coming down, fell in the kind of fluffy flakes which look nice on greeting cards but nowhere else. The insurance office and funeral supply company closed an hour before Jimmy Frank and Herm arrived. In the window, an open gold casket, bathed by an overhead spotlight, displayed a cream-colored satin diamond tucked interior.

"That's a fine looking casket," Herm Taylor said. "Casket like that gives you a good send-off. I don't care who you are, any man alive would be proud to lay in something like that."

"Don't talk to me about caskets, Herm," Jimmy Frank said. "Keep your head in the game."

"I'm just saying it's a nice looking casket," Herm said. "I wouldn't mind a casket look like that one."

Marvel and Arthur Johnson were upstairs. The

men could see them through the front window. Jimmy Frank and Herm Taylor would wait for the two brothers to exit before entering the building. Everything was ready.

Fontana was late.

Both Jimmy Frank and Herm Taylor were tired of waiting. They were tired of standing in the cold and snow.

* * *

Twenty cold minutes later, Phil Fontana still hadn't arrived.

Herm Taylor lighted a Kool cigarette. A gray Cadillac Fleetwood waited by the curb.

"You sure you both said tonight?" Herm said.

Jimmy Frank looked at Herm. What kind of question was that?

Herm Taylor looked nervous. Jimmy Frank found that troubling.

Herm wasn't nearly as smooth as he was when selling shoes at Thom McAn.

Still, Herm had done the reconnaissance.

Herm knew exactly where everything in the office lay.

Jimmy Frank looked at Herm. Herm shifting his feet.

"Maybe Fontana isn't coming," Herm said, "Maybe he decided to back his ass out."

Jimmy Frank watched Herm Taylor smoking. Nervous little puffs.

Herm was acting like a first-timer.

"Fontana's your man," Jimmy Frank said. "You were the one suggested him. I followed your advice, Herm. I talked him into working this job."

"You asked me for a safe-cracker. I gave you the name of a safe-cracker," Herm Taylor said.

Herm stamped his feet.

"Listen," he said. He pointed at the brick building.

Two big men had clumped down the interior steps of the building. They walked out of the building, one in front of the other. The men's steps were coordinated. Metronomic. Left. Right. Left.

They wore long dark overcoats, dark fedoras, scarves.

End-of-business day talk.

"Damn," Herm said. "That's how they ride?"

Herm Taylor nodded his head.

"Brothers Johnson" Herm said, "Live and in person."

"You know which one's which?" Herm said.

"Man with the moustache is Arthur," Jimmy Frank said.

"Insurance money," Herm said. "Lotta money in insurance."

"Unh-uh," Jimmy Frank said. "You still think they sell insurance, Herm?"

* * *

Phil Fontana was a half an hour late. Closer to an

hour.

"Surprise," he said.

He held a battered leather Gladstone in his right hand.

Herm jumped. Jimmy Frank shook his head.

"You're late," Jimmy Frank said. "We starting to think you weren't coming."

Fontana laughed. A *you're-putting-me-on* laugh.

"You two look suspicious as hell standing in the shadows."

Jimmy Frank studied Fontana.

"We been waiting. They left a while ago."

"Then I'm on time," Fontana said. "We had to wait for them, didn't we?"

"Let's go in," Jimmy Frank said.

Fontana pointed at the building.

"Gimme a second. I'll get us in the side door. I gotta take a look just in case there's some kind of alarm he doesn't know about. Don't mind the mess I'm going to make of the job. I wanna make it look like the work of an amateur. When I get my hands on the Diebold safe though, that'll be different. I'll open that one clean."

Fontana held up his hands.

"Everybody gloved up?"

Jimmy Frank and Herm held out their hands. They had both worn leather gloves. Fontana tossed light blue surgical gloves to both men.

"Put these on before you go in," Fontana said. "Much, much safer. You want, I got some powder to put on before, although you don't need it unless you got a latex allergy. Not uncommon, but I'll leave that up to you. Still, whatever you decide, you need to avoid touching things."

* * *

"Your job here is to keep watch, not look over my shoulder," Fontana said.

Fontana held a pair of needle nosed pliers in one hand, a small drill in the other. He had put on heavy glasses with magnification lenses mounted on their sides. Barking orders like a drill sergeant.

"Jimmy Frank stay down at the bottom of the stairs. Herman, you stand over there. Anyone comes in here, I want time to leave. And I mean leave with my equipment. This gear isn't cheap and it's getting hard to find. If anyone comes in, you create a diversion. I go straight out the door. With my bag. Remember that. I'm the one got the incriminating evidence. If you two get caught, the worst charge you can come up on is simple trespass, and I got a guy who can get you out of jail on any kind of charge like that before you even know you're in."

Herm muttered.

"Man's got everything figured out, don't he?"

The three men stood in Arthur Johnson's office. Dark striped wallpaper hung on the walls in front of Johnson's desk. Two matching leather upholstered wing chairs with reading lamps stood in two corners of the room.

Herm went over to one of the chairs and sat down.

"Guess one of these chairs is Marvel's and the other one's Arthur's."

Jimmy Frank smiled. He clicked open a humidor on the desk and helped himself to a cigar. Looked up.

Fontana was shaking his head.

"Not what we're here for," Fontana said. He was working his way along the wall of the office, tapping with his gloved middle knuckle as he went.

The speed with which Fontana had entered the building and disabled the alarm had amazed Jimmy Frank.

Jimmy Frank tucked the cigar into his shirt pocket. Headed toward the staircase.

"I got it," Fontana said.

He used both hands to take the picture down from the wall. The picture was of a lighthouse at either sunrise or sunset. Golden light poured through purple clouds. Behind the picture was the wall safe.

"Looks like a pretty standard situation here," Fontana said. "What we're looking at is a Diebold and this particular model isn't seen much any more. Maybe in Old Mexico you might see it, but this particular one goes back a ways. You say they run poker games?"

He reached into the Gladstone and took out a stethoscope and hung it over his neck.

"Just call me Young Doctor Kildare. Nothing to worry about now. Everything's working," he said. "It's a nice little take," Fontana said. "Not a life-changer, but not bad for a night's work."

The door of the Diebold was open. Fontana turned on the light on the desk to get a better look.

❊ ❊ ❊

Jimmy Frank peered into the safe to make sure the Diebold was empty and Fontana wasn't leaving part of the take in the safe. The safe was empty.

The money was on the desk.

There was a hell of a lot more than the money the men owed Jimmy Frank. He didn't want the extra, though. He would take the amount the brother's owed him. He pointed at the rest of the money then looked at Herm and Fontana.

"Crazy Phil," he said. "Enough there for the Lincoln?"

Fontana was going through the bills with his gloved hands.

"More than enough," Fontana said. "This is one helluva big score."

Jimmy Frank moved around him. Picked eight hundred dollar bills from the stack.

"I'll come around tomorrow, sign paperwork."

He looked at Phil and Herm.

"Close the place up nice when you leave."

MITCH WALCZAK

Mitch Walczak felt like his camel's hair toggle jacket gave him a European look of casual sophistication. He wore the knit Browns cap down over his ears on account of it was still cold as Billy be damned out here. It felt funny doing a delivery job for Hal, but Hal was paying, so why not?

Hal had been a different guy since he got back from Tucson. Something had happened to him out there. It was the kind of thing Mitch couldn't quite put his finger on, but he also knew it wasn't something he wanted to push too hard with Hal.

"No problem," Mitch said. "I gotta have the guy sign something or anything?"

Hal shook his head.

"Unh-uh," he said. "It's a simple delivery. Just check the address. Then make sure it's the guy. Not the housekeeper. Don't give it to her."

"Roger that," Mitch said. "Leave it to old Mitch."

* * *

Hank Standish looked at his watch. Two hours before Hilda would be getting off her plane at

Hopkins. The house looked fine. There was just the one thing, and Gerry Joyce had called him about that.

"Good news, Hank, old boy," Gerry said. "You can expect a package tonight. Don't say I never done nothing for you because I have. And it will arrive before six o'clock. You can set your watch."

This was good news, but still, it was almost time to go to the airport, and the package hadn't arrived.

* * *

Van Aken Boulevard was festooned with Christmas lights. Nothing too gaudy. Everything understated. Mitch Walczak liked this part of town. He hummed a bar of *Winter Wonderland*.

His sister lived somewhere near here with the fancy schmancy lawyer who Mitch sometimes worked for when he wasn't in the doghouse.

He checked the Van Aken address twice, just to be sure. He had the right house, all right.

The guy who met him at the front door took the package from Mitch and pulled out a five dollar bill and handed it to Mitch. Mitch thought the guy looked like he was about to cry, but in a good way.

"Merry Christmas," Mitch said. "I mean it."

CALIFORNIA

Conn Rutherford had taken off early from Easy Al's, which was good as far as Jackie was concerned. Jackie didn't want to hear any lectures from Conn about Phil Fontana or anything else.

Jackie was waiting for Fontana to pull up with Jerry Lalonde. Jackie had told Fontana he would do one job and see how it went.

He didn't look forward to working with Jerry Lalonde at all, even though he had to admit the man's hot wiring ability was impressive.

Jackie looked around the shack. Everything in here belonged to Conn. The Montgomery Ward heater. The sawed off shotgun. The pinned up photo of Shelly Fabares.

Conn wanted to look out for Jackie. Jackie couldn't fault the guy for that.

Did Conn know Jackie knew his little secret?

Jackie knew there was no Easy Al. Conn owned the place. Jackie had seen the title to Easy Al's the same time he'd seen Conn's license.

Albert Cornelius Rutherford.
Mentor-on-the-Lake, Ohio
DBA: Easy Al's Parking

The place was all Conn's.

Conn was loaded. He didn't have to sit out here in a freezing shack all winter. He just liked it.

* * *

The woman pulled her Volare into the lot.

Jackie came out of the shack to get her keys and to park the car.

She was the same woman who had gone into Eddie Swanson's the other night. She had come out just a few minutes later.

Her name was Louise. Jackie remembered he'd given her his name, too.

She was a classy looking woman. The kind of woman who went to Eddie Swanson's.

"I'll take those for you," Jackie said. He reached for her keys.

"I'm not parking," she said. "I came down here to ask you out."

Jackie looked at her. She did look like Mary Tyler Moore.

She could turn the world on with her smile.

"Right now?" he said. "You're asking me out? Like on a date?"

"That's what I was thinking," she said. "Right now."

Jackie turned back and looked at the shack.

He could put the bar down over the entrance.

Drop the *Sorry We're Closed* sign.

Conn wouldn't care.

He thought about Phil Fontana and Jerry Lalonde.

The hell with them. Conn was right. If Jackie started working for Fontana, eventually he would land in prison.

He turned to Louise.

"Where you thinking about going?" he said.

He wasn't dressed for any place nice, but maybe they could go to his place first and he could change.

"I was thinking about California," Louise said.

"Sounds good," Jackie said. "You want me to drive?"

EGGY

Eggy put the telephone down.

He looked out the leaded window of his Alhambra apartment. Somebody had built a snowman across the street. It made Eggy feel even more sad. The phone call from Hal Bailey had explained some things, but Eggy was still unhappy.

He didn't want to believe the part about Natasha. As a matter of fact, he *didn't* believe the part about Natasha.

Maybe she wasn't from Russia, but she was Russian. She was still intelligent. She was still exotic.

It was Natasha's uncle who was the problem. Probably the uncle sold Hal Bailey a bill of goods.

Telling Hal stories about Natasha.

What was the name Hal used? Susan.

Well, there was more to the story than the one Hal reported.

Hal even sounded apologetic about the money.

But it wasn't the money which concerned Eggy. It had never been the money. If he had to, Eggy would find out the truth for himself. He'd hired Hal to protect Natasha. And Hal was saying

Natasha, or Susan, was in on the scheme herself.

Eggy didn't believe Hal.

When he told Hal he didn't believe him, Hal didn't try to convince him.

"Suit yourself," Hal said. "It's your money."

Then he hung up the phone.

Outside, the snow had stopped for now. There were two cars parked in front of the Alhambra. Both were covered in white from the last snow. Eggy went into his small kitchen. Took out a wine glass and the bottle of cranberry juice. He wouldn't bother with ice.

There were two cans of Dinty Moore in the cupboard.

He went back to the window.

The phone rang. Eggy looked at it. Surprised. He didn't get very many phone calls and the last one from Hal had been depressing.

"Hi Eggy," Natasha said.

Her voice was smooth and the Slavic tones made Eggy feel warm.

"I found out about your uncle," Eggy said. "I was worried about you."

Natasha laughed.

"No reason to worry about me, Eggy," she said. "It is darling of you though, to care."

"I care about you," he said. "They said your name was Susan, not Natasha."

Natasha snorted.

"My parents," she said. "They say you need American name. Like Natalie Wood, okay? You know the big movie star? They say Susan is American as you can find. You know, like Suzy Q?"

"I knew you could explain, Natasha," Eggy said.

"Good news," Natasha said. "You remember I told you about my uncle's brother?"

"Your *other* uncle?" Eggy said.

"*Da*... I mean yes," Natasha said. "My other uncle. This one's named Vanya. You will like him. He's very sporty. Good news is he's going to be here and he will be loaded down with diamonds. Bottom line, Eggy, we just need to be more careful, please. And stay away from those crazy men who came to the tea room. So, long story short, my uncle Sergei, he left town, but my other uncle is coming here."

"When can we get together?" Eggy said.

Outside, a UPS delivery man was walking toward the Alhambra.

A new year was coming. A new month. Everything would start over.

Things would be better than they ever had been before.

A warm feeling of elation spread through Eggy's body.

Life felt worth living again.

"Maybe in January?" Natasha said.

HAL AND ANGIE

The bell jangled when Hal went into the flower shop in front of Higbees. The snow had stopped and the temperature had warmed since yesterday. There would be slush on the roads, not ice. This wasn't spring yet, but it was something.

The man Hal had seen the first time he went into the flower shop was fussing with another arrangement. Hal waited until the man came up to the counter.

❋ ❋ ❋

What kind of flowers do you bring for New Years?

Hal remembered Louise saying the man's name was Larry Carmichael.

"Hi Larry," Hal said. "Is Louise on break?"

"Oh my God, if only she were," Larry said. "She just left out of the clear blue sky. No two week notice, no nothing.

Larry sniffed.

"Is that a cologne you're wearing?" he said.

Hal nodded.

"English Leather," he said. "I hope I didn't go too

heavy with it. I got a date and sometimes it's hard to gauge."

"No," Larry said, "It's fine. Kind of a throwback, you know? I do that sometimes. Anyway, Louise is gone, and she didn't leave much of a vacancy."

"Thanks," Hal said. "Well still, I came in for flowers."

"Flowers we got," Larry said. "Just please don't say hostas."

✳ ✳ ✳

Angie Mandarich liked the roses Hal brought.

Larry even gave Hal a discount.

"They're leftovers from a wedding," Larry said. "That little piece of information can be just between you and me."

✳ ✳ ✳

Angie loved the Swabian Club.

"Oh my God, Hal," she said, "I've always wanted to come here. Stan and Ted sometimes come here. This place is so cool."

He ordered her a whiskey sour, figuring she must like them since she made them for Hal at the Tender Trap.

"Stan loves you," Angie said. "I don't know what the two of you did, but Stan said he had a blast."

Hearing this pleased Hal. Having Stan

Mandarich on his side could only be a good thing.

Over dinner, Hal told Angie about Hank Standish, Louise Atkinson, and the Wedgwood tiara.

"That's a crazy story," Angie said. "You think it was really hers? I mean Marie Antoinette's?"

Hal shook his head.

"Possibly," he said. "I told Louise what I needed to tell her. But who can say for sure? There's a lot of stuff in this world we'll never know."

December 28, 2022
Erie, Pennsylvania

BOOKS BY THIS AUTHOR

Trinity Works Alone

Trinity Thinks Twice

Trinity And The Short-Timer

Trinity Springs Forward

Trinity And The Heisters

Trinity Takes Flight

Ferguson's Trip

Lefty And The Killers

Ten Shots Quick And Other Stories Of
The New West

Dim Lights Thick Smoke

Thanks to John Holliday for designing the covers of my books. Also, thanks to Carolyn Holliday for editing them.

Thank you for reading *The Forest City.*

If you enjoyed reading *The Forest City*, please consider writing a short review on Amazon and telling your friends.

As Walter Tevis, writer of *The Hustler* and *The Queen's Gambit* wrote when making the same request: "word of mouth is an author's best friend and much appreciated. "

Trevor Holliday

Made in the USA
Las Vegas, NV
19 August 2024

94118639R00100